ALONE

ALONE

MEGAN E. FREEMAN

ALADDIN
New York   London   Toronto   Sydney   New Delhi

ALADDIN

An imprint of Simon & Schuster Children's Publishing Division
1230 Avenue of the Americas, New York, New York 10020
First Aladdin hardcover edition January 2021
Text copyright © 2021 by Megan E. Freeman
Jacket illustration copyright © 2021 by Pascal Campion
All rights reserved, including the right of reproduction in whole or in part in any form.
ALADDIN and related logo are registered trademarks of Simon & Schuster, Inc.
For information about special discounts for bulk purchases, please contact
Simon & Schuster Special Sales at 1-866-506-1949 or business@simonandschuster.com.
The Simon & Schuster Speakers Bureau can bring authors to your live event.
For more information or to book an event contact the Simon & Schuster Speakers
Bureau at 1-866-248-3049 or visit our website at www.simonspeakers.com.
Jacket designed by Heather Palisi
Interior designed by Mike Rosamilia
The text of this book was set in Minion Pro.
Manufactured in the United States of America 0822 FFG
10 9 8 7 6
Library of Congress Control Number 2020946086
ISBN 9781534467569 (hc)
ISBN 9781534467583 (ebook)

Excerpt on pages 362–363: "The Summer Day" from *House of Light* by Mary Oliver, published by Beacon Press, Boston. Copyright © 1990 by Mary Oliver, used herewith by permission of the Charlotte Sheedy Literary Agency, Inc.

Excerpt on page 360: *The Poems of Emily Dickinson*, edited by Thomas H. Johnson, Cambridge, Massachusetts: The Belknap Press of Harvard University Press. Copyright © 1951, 1955, 1979, 1983 by the President and Fellows of Harvard College.

for Fiona Grace

. . . the sound of a human voice.
There is no sound like this in all the world.

—Scott O'Dell, *Island of the Blue Dolphins*

This Is Not Adolescent Hyperbole

This is my reality.

Alone in this place
where I've been
surviving on my own
for over three years
with no one but
a big, smelly
rottweiler who farts
and hogs the covers.

(You might think
I'm exaggerating but
I'm not. I'm not just
"being dramatic," like
my grandma might say.)

I figured by the time
I was a teenager I'd be
thinking about
getting my driver's permit
going to dances
playing varsity soccer
and kissing.
But instead

1

I'm thinking about
where to find food
and fuel
and water
and whether to use Mountain Dew
to force flush the toilet
or to drink
even though it's the color
of radioactive urine
and it's probably toxic
when ingested over
long periods of time.

Better to be radioactive
or dehydrated?
These are the questions
that plague
my daily existence.

At least for now.

At least
until
my parents
come back.

Heaven

(n.) bliss, ecstasy, paradise, dreamland

Back When My Life Was Heaven and I Had No Idea

"Shoes off before you come in!"
Mom hollers as I open the kitchen door.
"I mopped today."
She wipes orange slop off the baby's face.
"Honey, I know you have different rules
at your dad's, but could you try
a little harder to make an effort
when you're at our house?"

Sometimes
the way my mom talks to me
feels like a scratchy shirt tag
on the back of my neck.

I kick off my tattered silver Converse
and calculate how much more
I need to save before
I can special-order a custom pair
for my thirteenth birthday.

Mom hugs me.
"Sorry, sweetie.
I'm just rushing to get ready to go.

So glad you're home."
Hands me a mug filled with
chopped carrots and celery.
"I bet you're starving."

I squeeze an empty Twinkie wrapper in my pocket.
I'll have to remember to throw it away later.

Before middle school
I was never even tempted to lie.
Lately though
it just seems to make things
so much simpler.

Mom

"Are you going out like that?"
I make my horror obvious.

Mom has on the paisley embarrassments
she calls her "meditation pants."
She always wears something mortifying
to the Tuesday-night dharma talks.

They all just sit still and
learn to breathe.
Like breathing is something
you have to learn.

Mom does that thing
where she pulls my hair
to get me to smile.
"Oh come on, honey.
It's called a 'sitting meditation.'
If I wore jeans like yours
I'd lose circulation in my legs.
Come to think of it
did your dad see you wearing those
when you left this morning?"

Seriously?
My jeans are not even tight.
So what if the shape
of my cell phone
is permanently embossed
on one pocket?

Sometimes just being
in the same room with my mom
even the sound of her voice
makes it hard to be a person.

Paul's car pulls up.
Mom grabs her wallet
out of the diaper bag.
"Thanks for babysitting, sweetie.
We should be back early
unless they're stopping people
at the checkpoints.
We'll definitely be home
before the curfew."

She kisses Trevor.
Calls to the twins.
"Hey, guys, bedtime at
the usual time tonight.
No messing around!"

She signs *I love you*
toward the dining room
blows me a kiss
and is gone.

Brothers

Trevor smiles from his high chair.
Reaches for me.

I lean in.
Pretend to steal his nose.
He erupts in belly laughs.
Smears pureed carrots in my long hair.
I pull it into a ponytail with
a twist tie.
Sigh.

I adore my baby brother
but
I want to get upstairs.
Check on The Weekend Plan.

"You couldn't pay me enough to eat that."
Elliott surprises me.
Unnaturally quiet.
Never hear him coming.

I try to bribe him to feed Trevor.
(I have another Twinkie
in my backpack.
In the gluten-free economy

of my bizarre family
Twinkies are worth a lot
on the stepbrother
black market.)

But he's helping James.
Science project.
Can't be bought.
They have one of those
freaky twin connections.
Can read each other's minds.

Plus the fact that James is deaf
makes me feel awkward.
Even after all this time.
I know it's not cool
to say that, but there it is.
I said it anyway.

Doesn't help I live half-time
with Dad and Jennifer.
I used to love the regular breaks
from gluten-phobic diets and
silent dinner conversations.

Until Paul and Mom had Trevor.
Now it feels like I'm missing out.

I want my own freaky connection
with someone who can read my mind.

Pocket vibrates.
Click on Ashanti's name.

6:55 p.m.
WEEKEND MISSION IS GO

Our Weekend Plan
(or, How I Got Myself into This Mess)

We are going
to lie
to our parents
and have
a
secret sleepover.

Emma and Ashanti
will say
they are spending
the night at
each other's house
and I will tell Mom
I am with Dad
and tell Dad
I am with Mom
but
we will actually
sleep over at
my grandparents' empty
summer apartment.

We will:
  make popcorn
  stay up super late
  watch glamorous old Katharine Hepburn movies
  lounge on the king-sized bed
  sleep as long as we like

No one nagging us to:
  get up
  do the laundry
  clean your room
  change (stinky gross) diapers

We. Are. Geniuses.

Thesis

After dinner, Elliott sneaks up on me again.
"Can you please help me with my book report?
I'm having trouble with my thesis."

Thesis?
He's in fourth grade.
What does he know about drafting a thesis?

"I'm in Accelerated."

(my family is a freak show)

He takes a deep breath.
Launches his explanation.

"It's called *Island of the Blue Dolphins*
and it's about a girl who lives alone
on an island for eighteen years.
She jumps off a boat and stays behind
to save her brother but then he dies
and she tames a dog and later she makes a friend
but really she's pretty much on her own
until she's totally grown up and—"

"ELLIOTT."
Sharper than I intend.

His hands flutter.
He shifts his weight.
I tweak the brim of his hat.
He relaxes.

"I have to prove whether her biggest challenge is to
      A. defend herself against the wild dogs
      B. provide food and shelter for herself
                or
      C. learn to trust a friend."

Plot details are sketchy in my memory.
I ask him what he thinks.

"Her brother dies and she's left alone."
Elliott's eyes fill with tears.
"The wild dogs get him."
He glances toward the dining room
where we hear James working.

Jeez. Why do they let little kids read stuff like this
even if they are in Accelerated?

"Listen, Ell," I say, "wild dogs can be scary for sure
and it sucks what happens to her brother

but if she doesn't have a place to live and
food to eat, she can't exactly survive, can she?
I think her biggest challenge is B, definitely."

Elliott exhales.
"Really? I kind of thought so too
but I wasn't positive. Thanks, Maddie!"

I smile.
And think of the upcoming weekend.
Our very own *Island of No Brothers or Parents*.
All alone with unlimited fun and freedom.

Cannot wait.

Paul

I wrangle the boys into their bunk beds.

Trevor finishes his bottle and falls
asleep in the crib across the room
from where I lie on my own twin bed.

I don't love sharing my room
but at least for now he's quiet.

Log in to my laptop.
Kitten videos.
Tumbling around on
a patient golden retriever.
Adorable. So precious.

Hear garage door.
Switch computer to online history textbook.
Open binder.
Stretch out on stomach.
Pretend to study.

After a few minutes, Paul peeks in the open door.

"Hey there, how's it going, kiddo?"
He crosses to Trevor's crib.
Tucks in the baby blanket.

I grunt.

Frown at my Cornell notes.

Draw an elephant in the margin.

(My friends all say I draw really good elephants.)

Paul tries again.

"It's nice to have you here. We miss you

on the weeks you're at your dad's."

Not even sure why I'm being so rude.

Paul's gentle voice brings out the meanest part of me.

"Well, we really appreciate you babysitting

so we could have a little date. Thanks."

He pauses.

A few awkward moments.

I keep drawing.

"Okay. Sleep tight."

Paul leaves the room.

Closes the door.

exhale

slam the computer shut

roll onto my back

stare up at the ceiling fan
trace the pattern of blades moving in lazy rotations

weekend can't come soon enough

Friday

Feeling fine.
New striped top and denim leggings.
Jean jacket. Floral backpack.
I even let Mom kiss me
as I leave for school.

Language Arts
(autopilot)
Pre-Algebra
(autopilot)
Study Hall
(shopping list)
Social Studies
(lockdown drill)
Fine Art
(progress on vanishing-point project)
Spanish
(autopilot)
Earth Science
(autopilot)
Final bell!

Bike to store.
(snacks, soda, frozen pizza)
Grocery bags on handlebars.

Fifteen-minute wait at intersection for
military trucks to roll through town.

Convoys come through every day now.
Mom always has the news on
listening for information
about checkpoints and delays
and "protective action" curfews
whatever that means.

I personally don't get why everyone is so uptight.
It's just a bunch of trucks moving stuff around
not World War III.

Pedal to grandparents' empty apartment.
(Easy to get the key
since Dad had an extra set
hanging on a hook
in the laundry room.)

Soda in fridge to chill.
TV on.
Feet up.

YES

Tangled Web

to Mom 4:46 p.m.

plan changed

staying over at dads for help with huge history project

back tomorrow afternoon xo

to Dad 4:47 p.m.

babysitting tonight for P and Mom

c u sunday after church? I'll make the waffles this
time!

from Mom 4:50 p.m.

Please ask Dad if he might be able to get us two tickets to the
concert next Thursday? I'd like to take Paul for his birthday.

Good luck with the project and don't stay up too late. ☺

Concert tickets are a good idea.

Dad conducts.

Jennifer plays flute.

Paul doesn't play anything

but loves music.

from Dad 4:53 p.m.

Sounds good. I want bananas and walnuts on mine! Make sure you charge Paul time and a half for working on a weekend! ha ha.

love you.

Everything is going perfectly.

Monkey Wrench

Emma 6:40 p.m.

no sleepover.

ashanti threw up in her moms car ☹

Me 6:40 p.m.

gross! can u still come?

tell ur mom ur sleeping over at my house

Emma 6:41 p.m.

tried but she called ur mom who said u were 2 busy w/ur dad
doing history. sux! maybe next week?

Me 6:41 p.m.

A banquet of junk food spans the coffee table.
All that money and risk and
no one's coming after all.

At least there's no crying baby to wake me up
and I can sleep in tomorrow.

I settle into the couch and scroll through channels
until I find an old black-and-white movie.

Ginger Rogers tap-dances with Fred Astaire
around a big empty dance studio.
An invisible orchestra plays somewhere offscreen.
Ginger lifts her wrist and her skirt swirls around her
like the petals of a tropical flower.
Her perfect hair falls to her shoulders
in smooth, elegant waves.

I tug my fingers through my curly tangles
and reach for a Twinkie.

Disruption

middle of the night
trucks rumble
loud voices outside

grab remote
TV off

glad lights aren't on in the apartment

something BANGS against the front door
I jump

footsteps move down the hall
unfamiliar voice speaks
outside the door

"What about this one?"

"They're part-timers," says a neighbor
"only here for summers and holidays."

voices move away
doors close and open
and close

I creep across the floor
crouch by the door
hear people talking downstairs
dogs barking outside
someone having a party?
curious
but can't risk being seen

avoid windows
sound
light

if I get caught here alone
I'll be grounded forever
worry infects the room

eventually sounds fade
crawl back to the couch
pull up Grandma's afghan

sit in the dark

        wide awake

Forsaken

(adj.) deserted; abandoned; forlorn

Saturday

Bright sun shines
high in the sky.

The sofa cushion is embossed on my cheek
and my teeth feel fuzzy.
I rub sleep crumbs from my eyes.
Reach for the last of the popcorn.
Plug in my phone to charge the dead battery.

Messages and missed calls light up the screen.

Oh crap.

Text Message

⚠ EMERGENCY ALERTS **12:01 a.m.**

IMMINENT THREAT ALERT. INCREASED PROTECTIVE ACTIONS ARE BEING TAKEN. FOLLOW INSTRUCTIONS OF LOCAL AUTHORITIES. THIS IS NOT A DRILL.

VOICE MAIL FROM DAD

"Hey there, sweetheart. I'm sorry this happened so fast and we didn't get a chance to touch base, but we'll reconnect when we arrive, and then your mom and I will work out a plan for the next few weeks, okay? In the meantime, don't be scared, I'm sure this is all just precautionary. And Jennifer says not to worry, because she's packing your earbuds and your purple jeans, and she'll give them to you when we see you. Okay, Peanut? I love you and I'll see you soon. Be sure to help your mom with the boys and try not to worry. Bye now."

1:39 a.m.

VOICE MAIL FROM MOM

"Hi, darlin', it's Mom. I hope you can hear me over Trevor crying. I was really hoping to talk to you, but I imagine things over there are as crazy as they are here. We're trying to get everyone up and moving and it's pretty chaotic. Listen, I only have a second, but I want you to be sure to stay with your dad and don't try to come home. It's too hectic to try to make a switch now, and I worry that we'll end up separated in all the confusion. Stay with Dad and Jennifer, and we will meet you all when we get there. Okay, Maddie? I love you with all my heart, and I can't wait to see you. Tell your dad I'll call him."

2:07 a.m.

VOICE MAIL FROM MOM

"Hi, sweets, it's Mom again. We were going to drive ourselves, but it sounds like that's not an option so it looks like we'll be on one of the transports. I can't get through to your dad, but hopefully we'll connect at the embarkation point. If not, we'll see you when we arrive, okay? Try not to worry, baby. I love you!"

2:21 a.m.

Text Messages

Emma 2:30 a.m.

Thank god we didnt end up sleeping over! isnt this freaky?! which transport r u on? call me!!

Ashanti 3:03 a.m.

hey girl!!! im scared out of my mind and i cant believe we got so lucky imagine if we hadnt been home????we r in line for #78 but the guy says its full so i dont know if we'll get on where r u? i hope we r on the same transport!

W
H
A
T

IS

H
A
P
P
E
N
I
N
G
?

Panic

Speed-dial. Mom. Now.

Voice mail. (damn)
"Mom? Where are you?
What's happened?
I wasn't at Dad's last night.
I stayed alone at Grandma's.
Call me back, please, Mom?
I'm really worried!"

SPEEDDIALDADNOW.

Voice mail.
"Daddy, it's Maddie please call me right away
I don't know what's going on and I'm scared
please call me, Dad!"

Emma:
Voice mail.

Ashanti:
Voice mail.

I
text
text
text
text
text
text
everyone.

Nothing.

Television

Reach for remote.
Grave-faced news anchor talks to camera.

"... imminent threat resulting in emergency
evacuations ... state of emergency ... top
priority to secure the homeland ... infrastructure
protection ... western United States ... information
security ... crisis and emergency planning ..."

TV shows farmland.
Soldiers erecting rows and rows of tents.
Highways and traffic jams for miles.

Picture changes.

Hundreds of sleepy-looking people
standing in lines waiting
climbing into military buses
vans, trains, trucks.

I scan the crowds
for family or friends but
don't recognize anyone.
Don't even know if
I'm looking at images
from Colorado.

Grave-faced news anchor continues.

". . . national threat advisory . . . others
on pre-evacuation alert . . . temporary
shelters in multiple jurisdictions . . . reduce
vulnerability . . . the safety of American
citizens . . . stay tuned for more
up-to-the-minute coverage of Operation
Relocate Freedom . . ."

Grave-faced news anchor disappears
and a cartoon dog barks at a whale
on the screen.

I drop to my knees
crawl to the window
peer over the sill.

No one is in the parking lot below.
No one is swimming in the pool.
No cars or traffic pass by on the street.

I don't see a single person.

Imminent Threat?

What kind of threat?
Are we under attack?
Am I in danger?

Everything looks normal outside
except for the absence
of human beings.

What sort of threat are they talking about?
Why can't they be specific?

I've got to get out of here.
I've got to find my family.

Is it safe?
I've got to find out, either way.

I turn away from the window
and reach for my shoes.

At the Last Minute

I think about air.
What if the imminent threat is in the air?
Some kind of poison?

Should I be breathing?
How can I not breathe?

I grab Grandpa's red bandana
off the brim of his gardening hat.
Unroll it. Tie it around my face
so I look like a surgeon
from a Wild West sci-fi movie.

I make my way out into the hallway
and sniff.

I don't smell anything except
for Grandpa's aftershave.

Downstairs outside
I cling to the sides of the building.
Peek around the corner.

Nothing.

The sun is warm.
A breeze blows a piece of junk mail
across the parking lot.
Birds are singing.

Singing birds need to breathe!
Maybe no poison?

I take a shallow breath
and run for my bike.

Evidence

I pedal down the street
toward the center of town.

I ride around clothing
photo albums, potted plants
alarm clocks, baby toys, framed pictures
laptop cases, cell phone chargers
sleeping bags.

I come to the parking lot
for the Park-n-Ride on the corner
by the megachurch.
Half-packed suitcases
lie open on the sidewalks.

This must be where they loaded
everyone onto the transports.
What did Mom call it?
The embarkation point?

If the streets and sidewalks are any
indication, it looks like people
had to leave a lot of belongings behind.

I coast around the street searching
for any signs of anyone.

Hello?

      Anyone here?

            Hello?

HELLO? CAN ANYONE HEAR ME?

I get off my bike and
turn in circles.
I scan every direction
for movement of any kind.

Sounds come
from the bus shelter.

I run
hoping
someone
is
still

there.

Place Compromised Devices Here

At the shelter
labeled cardboard barrels
overflow with
cell phones.

I hear a ringtone.

Run from one barrel
to the next
dig inside to find
the ringing phone.

It stops.

All I can
hear
is my own
desperate
panting.

I sit down
on the hard pavement
surrounded by cell phones
and abandoned luggage.

I cry.

A Thought So Terrible

I dig my own phone out of my pocket.
Speed-dial Mom.
It rings in my ear.

A few seconds later
Scott Joplin's "The Entertainer"
—Mom's special ringtone for me—
comes from one of the barrels.
I cry out.

Eyes blurring and breath shallow
I speed-dial Dad.

A barrel rings.

I dial Paul.
     And Jennifer.
        And Emma.
        And Ashanti.

            The barrels keep ringing.

All the cell phones
have been

left

behind.

Brain Churn

What now?
What now?
What now?

Bike twenty miles out to the interstate
and try to find someone?

Head north to the fire station
and hope emergency crews are still there?

Dial 911!

I hold my breath and pray
for a live person at the other end.

Eleven rings.

". . . you have reached a number
that has been disconnected . . . check
the number and dial again . . ."

I call my grandparents in Texas.

". . . abnormally heavy call volume . . . could
not be completed . . . try again . . ."

Grave-faced news anchor echoes in my head.
". . . temporary shelters in multiple jurisdictions . . ."

With all my heart I do not want to think
the next, horrible thought that moves
like a fast-growing cancer through my brain.

The thought thinks itself anyway.

What if
 my parents have been sent
 to different shelters
 in different places?

And what if
 they each still think
  I am with the other?

Without their cell phones
it could be days
—or even weeks—
before they realize

I've
been left
behind.

Upheaval

I ride through town, looking for any sign
of another human. Occasionally dogs bark
or a hungry cat runs across the road.

At Dad's, the front door stands open
and Jennifer's flutes are still in the house.

She never travels without her flutes.

I close the windows, lock the doors, and
slip the key into my pocket.

At Mom's, the minivan is in the driveway
with the sliding door and back hatch open.
Duffel bags and suitcases sit on the front porch.

It looks like Mom just stepped inside
and will be right back.

My heart leaps with hope
but I remember the ringing cell phones
in the barrels downtown.
I swallow tears. Close the car doors
and go inside.

In their rush to leave
they left a mess.

open cupboards
open closet doors
unmade beds
scattered clothes

in the boys' room
toppled baskets of toys
books piled in stacks

in my room
Trevor's empty crib
humidifier still steaming

I switch it off
curl up on my bed
clutch my tattered
Lovey Bunny.

Reality Check

Twenty-four hours ago
I sat in school
surrounded by
classmates
teachers
custodians.

I went to
the grocery store
and navigated
busy streets
full of traffic.

Horns honked
and people
shopped
biked
stood in line
ate ice cream
played in
the splash fountain.

Now
the only sounds
come from the house

or the natural world.
The refrigerator hums
birds sing
the house fan kicks on
but not a single car
helicopter
or plane.

No voices
out in the street.

No basketball dribbling
in the Nortons' driveway
next door.

No *kabump-kabump-kabump*
of a skateboarder
cruising over cracks
in the sidewalk.

Not a single human sound.

Just clocks ticking
and dogs barking.

      Dogs barking?

I remember cats
crossing the road and
dogs in yards
as I cycled home.

No one took their pets?

Surely the evacuation can't last long
or people would have taken their pets!

I have nothing to worry about.
People won't let their animals starve.
Everyone will be back in a day or two.

Dread runs off my body
like hot water circling
the shower drain.
Relief embraces me
like a warm terry-cloth towel.

Productivity

If my parents will be home in a few days
I might as well make myself useful.
And maybe make up for the fact
that I lied to them.

Boys' room:
    pick up toys from floor
    stack books on desks
    pile dirty clothes into hamper

Mom and Paul's room:
    make bed
    hang clothes in closets
    turn off lights

Bathrooms:
    clear counters
    close medicine chests
    wipe mirrors

Front porch:
    bring in duffels and suitcases
    water flowerpots

I find keys in the van's ignition.
Pull it back in the garage?

I've only ever driven
one time
at my uncle's ranch
in California.

Mom was pissed when she found out.

I lock the car
leave it in the driveway
close the garage door.

Heavy Call Volume

Every fifteen minutes, I call my grandparents
but still get the "heavy call volume" message.

I haven't eaten all day.
I flip on the radio in the kitchen
and hear the Car Guys
teasing a caller about his carburetor.
The familiar voices comfort me.

I find an apple
almond butter
a gluten-free mac-and-cheese dinner with soy cheese
but I'm so hungry I don't care.

A jingle plays and the news comes on.

What is the *imminent threat*?
How long will the evacuation last?

Reporters talk.
    "safeguard the American people
    the cooperation of patriots"
Descriptions of people
sleeping on cots
sitting in shelters

waiting in lines.
I listen for new information, but
no one makes any actual sense and
it just repeats what I've already heard
adding that "agencies across
the eastern half of the United States
are coordinating efforts
to take in displaced evacuees."

I chew my apple.

Could there really be something
right here
in Millerville, Colorado
that is a threat to me
personally?

First Night

The streetlights come on.
They glow faint orange at first
then gain strength.
I search the sky for clues
but only the evening star
flickers over the foothills
and the moon rises
on the horizon.
I cross to the sidewalk.
Look up and down
the street.

The neighborhood houses
line up in tidy rows.
Some have lights left on
in the windows.
Others are dark.
Carriage lights on timers
glow on either side
of garage doors.
It's almost
an ordinary evening
on Lake Drive.

To the west, the street dead-ends
at Miner's Lake Park.

How many times have I taken the boys
to the playground there or to rent
paddleboats in the summer?

How often have I pushed Trevor
in the infant swing while Mom went
for a quick run around the lake?

Those untroubled days
seem long ago
even though
it was only yesterday
I was left behind.

Somewhere up the block
a dog howls at the dusk.
From the other side of the lake
a coyote yips an answer.

I go back inside and
lock the door behind me.
Being alone is weird enough
but being alone at night is
giving me the creeps.

I lock every window and
close the curtains.
Barricade myself from
the ghost town
that is my neighborhood.

Upstairs in Mom and Paul's room
I turn on the TV.
Click and click.
"No signal"
on every channel.

Turn the cable box off
wait thirty seconds
on again
click over and
over
and
over and
over.
I give up.
Pull out *The Philadelphia Story*
with Katharine Hepburn.
Pop it in the player.
Escape into glamour
and style from
an earlier century.

I climb up into the big, soft bed.

Try
to forget
I am
completely
entirely
totally
alone.

Morning

Alarm
going off
going off
going off
going off.

Six a.m.
Mom gets up early to run.

Mom.

The nightmare of the last twenty-four hours
coagulates in my stomach and
I almost don't make it
to the bathroom in time.
Gluten-free/dairy-free vomit
swirls down the toilet.
The irony is not lost on me.

I curl up on the bathroom floor.
Cool tile comforts my cheek.

I stare at a clump of Mom's hair nested
in the corner behind the tank.
I want to save it, her DNA.

I might need it for cloning
someday, just in case.

    (in case I never see her again)

But I lie without moving
and
close my eyes.

I conjure the peaceful voice
from Mom's yoga video
and try to breathe into my belly
but
my belly's still clenched
too tightly around
my fear.

Refusing to let go.

Outside

Everything out the window
looks exactly like it did
last night.
No sign of anyone. Nothing
has moved.

Standing on the front porch
I hear birds singing at the lake.
A pair of swallows darts
in and around the eaves of the house.

Mother Nature doesn't seem to mind
an empty town with no people.

The sun still rises.
The swallows go right on
sculpting their muddy nest
high out of reach.

A sudden crash from next door
at the Nortons' house.
I pee my pants a tiny bit.

Someone's over there.

Next Door

I pound on the back door.

Silence.

I use the hidden spare key to
let myself in.

George, the Nortons' rottweiler,
eats chocolate chip cookies from
broken shards of cookie jar
on the kitchen floor.

He looks at me.
I tell him to stay and he does.

I sweep up the mess.
He sniffs around for another cookie.
I scratch between his ears and
he wags his stubby little nub of tail.

I fill a bowl with water and look for dog food.
George wags his whole rear end and keeps
bumping into me as I take out the can opener.
He gobbles every bite and finishes the water.
I rub his head and belly.

Poor baby.
No wonder he went for the cookie jar.

He gives me a little lick and whimpers.
He needs to go outside.

He jumps up and runs
to the back door.
He sniffs around the yard
while I tuck his bowls
into a grocery bag.
Add several cans of dog food
and some dog treats.
I find his leash in
the coat closet.

I whistle and he comes to me.
No need for us both to hang out alone.

He wags again and does his
doggy pant-smile thing. He nuzzles
his head under my hand.

Having company
feels better already.

Stay Put

George makes me braver.
More optimistic.
He runs happily alongside my bike.

We clean up the mess at Dad's house
then scout all over town looking for anyone
or for transports passing through.

We go to the Park-n-Ride and
post a big handwritten sign.
We hang around for a long time
hoping one of the phones might ring
hoping someone might call
might find me here alone
but
they are all running out of battery.

I keep trying my grandparents
and other friends and relatives
but no cell service yet.
I stay logged on to my computer
sending e-mails to everyone
but the little dial keeps spinning.
Looking for networks
Looking for networks
Looking for networks

I debate riding five miles
over to Lewistown or all the way
out to the interstate
to see if I can find anyone
but according to news reports
the entire state is evacuated.

And then there's Dad's
Golden Rule for Hiking and Camping:

> *If you're ever lost, STAY PUT.*
> *Ensure proper supplies*
> *for warmth through the night*
> *then wait for help to come to you.*

Technically, I'm not lost.
I know exactly where I am.
Is this a "stay put" time?

What if I leave to find help
and I do get lost or hurt
and everyone comes home
and finds me missing?

Following Dad's rule
seems like the smartest thing
at least for now.

I stay put.

Third Night

We curl up on Mom's bed
to binge-watch a boxed set
of *I Love Lucy*.

George takes over Paul's pillow.
Under normal circumstances
this would never be allowed
but I am prepared to
face the consequences.
He whimpers in his sleep.
Twitches his paws.
I lean on his broad back.
He grunts.
Exhales loudly.

Then the power goes out.

Television dies.
Lights switch off.
The whole house.
Silent and dark.

George lifts his head as I cross to the window.
I don't see anything *imminently threatening*.

Neighborhood is black.
Garage carriage lights are out.
And streetlights and
lights down the block at
the lake playground.

Only light is the faint white glow
of solar-powered garden lights lining
paths in neighboring yards.

George whines. Puts his head down.
His eyes follow my shape as I cross the room.

In the kitchen I find flashlight, candles, matches.
I light six candles in the wrought-iron
candleholder in the dining room.
I light votive candles in the living room.

Ambiance, Mom would call it.
A little candlelight to set the mood.
Every national crisis needs a little romance.

Dark

Outside, the moon hasn't yet begun to rise.
The constant glow in the skies above
Denver is gone.
The dark sky is clear and
stars shine loudly.

I haul a comforter into the backyard.
Pull the hammock stand to
the center of the grass.

George sniffs his way around the edges of the yard.
Explores dark corners. Nighttime smells.

Coyotes yip and cry over near the lake.

George perks up.
Gives a low growl in the back of his throat.
Trots to the fence.
Barks a warning.

I whistle and he comes to me, tall and alert.
I sway back and forth.

I remember long nights on backpacking trips
with Dad, high in the mountains and far
from the city's light pollution.

I locate Venus.
See the misty band of Milky Way
tearing a rip in the inky night.

I wish Dad were here
with his telescope and
his astronomy app
to identify
everything I'm seeing in the sky.

To help me pinpoint
exactly
where I am
in the universe.

Exploration

(n.) act of investigating; examination;
search for natural resources

Investigation

After the power outage
George and I conduct
a systematic investigation
of the entire town.
Street by street
across the grid.
Seeking any signs of life.
I bike slowly, listening.
George pads alongside
sniffing the air.

We visit homes of
friends and acquaintances.
Businesses and schools.
If we find pets, we coax them out
hoping they will scrounge food
to survive on their own.

At Millerville Middle School
we find an unlocked door
behind the gym.
Wander the halls.
Footsteps echo against
rows of lockers.
I dial my locker combination.

Stare at the contents.
Everything is just as I left it:
    sticky travel mug
    bunch of binders
    magnets of Frida Kahlo and Georgia O'Keeffe
    plaid scarf from last winter

I can hear my math teacher
droning on about lockers and how
they should be called permutation locks
not combination locks.
I wish I was in his class for real.
Happily bored and surrounded
by people I didn't even
realize I loved.

A few months ago
I would have jumped at the offer
of an indefinite vacation.
Now I long for
the predictable regularity of classes.
The comfort of having a daily routine.
A place to be and people to notice
when I'm absent.

We leave school and ride on
through parks, playgrounds

the entire length of the creek path.
Bubbles float downstream
and accumulate in yellow foam
along the shore.
George tries to drink but I stop him.
Getting sick with giardia
is the last thing we need.
I give him what's left from
my water bottle.

At the end of our search
all we have to show for it are
sore paws and sunburned shoulders.

I think of Emma and Ashanti.
How things would be different now
if only
they had been able to spend the night.

Without Power

The water stops running.

I lug bottled water
up from the basement.
Wonder about recycling
the empty bottles.

Toilets stop refilling and won't flush.

I remember once
when the water was off at Dad's
he flushed by pouring water
directly into the bowl.

I don't want to waste
drinking water
but I find a case of red wine
in the basement.

It's a fact that wine smells bad
and tastes worse.
Even if I liked it
my parents would murder me
if I started drinking alcohol
the minute I was left alone.

Pull out a bottle and am relieved
to find a screw cap
not a cork.
Break the seal and
pour a third of the bottle
into the toilet.

Nothing happens.

Maybe more volume? More speed?

I find a bucket
in the laundry room.
Fill it with wine.
I empty the whole bucket
into the toilet bowl
all at once.

The toilet flushes.

The sound is like music.

Waiting

We eat what fresh food we can.
Stuff what's left into garbage bags
before spoiled food
stinks up the whole house.
Drag the bags to the alley.
Throw them in the dumpster.

I lower the saddle on Mom's bike.
Use it to pull Trevor's bike trailer
to Dad's house.
I load up the camp stove, lantern
more bottles of water
a case of propane cylinders.
Haul it back to Mom's.

After two weeks
we finish the food in Mom's pantry.

Start on soup and
canned vegetables
from next door.
Use bottled water
to boil pasta. Oatmeal.

The days are long
so I don't light the lantern
or candles much.
I save resources and
time my activities with
the daylight.

But I tell myself my parents
are on their way home.

No One Comes

It's getting more difficult
to comfort myself with the belief
that my parents will be back any minute.

At night, I curl up against George's broad back.
I mull scenarios.
Imagine the reasons why no one has come for me.

The Best Explanation:
> My parents are in different shelters.
> They haven't yet been able to contact each other
> so they don't know I've been left behind.
> It will just be a matter of time before they
> reconnect and discover what happened.

I imagine the look on my parents' faces when
they realize where I am.
Mom will demand to talk to whoever is in charge
refusing to take no for an answer.
Dad can convince anyone to do anything.

It will only be a matter of time before they'll be here
maybe even in a big military Humvee that will drive right up
to the front of the house, honk the horn, and my parents will
climb down to embrace me and carry me away to safety.

That's the good scenario.

The bad scenario involves a transport accident
on the highway, far from help or hospitals.
My little brothers hurt and crying.
Mom bleeding on the side of the road.
Paul calling out for help.

Or Dad and Jennifer mangled with dozens of others
in an overturned truck, bodies scattered across the highway
like images on the news from faraway wars.

I banish those pictures from my mind
but they invade my dreams.
I thrash and cry out.
Wake with tears on my face.
George, concerned and whimpering.

On those long nights
I drag my blankets out to the hammock.
Watch the stars rove across the sky.
Rock myself back to troubled sleep.

Routine

As summer temperatures rise
we fall into a routine.
Spend our time in the cool comfort
of the basement family room.

At sunset, I bring in solar garden lights
I've collected from the neighborhood.
Place them in twos and threes throughout the house.
They illuminate enough to get around.
In the morning, I gather them up and
return them to the sunny backyard.
They recharge all day.

We have no shortage of good books.
I reread my childhood favorites.
E. B. White. Kate DiCamillo.
Roald Dahl. Natalie Babbitt.
The *Calvin and Hobbes* treasury.
Old friends to smooth the hard edges
of being frightened and alone.

Sometimes I read to myself.
Other times I read aloud to George.
He listens politely. Wags his tail when
I check to see if he's paying attention.

When we read late into the evening, we often hear
the howls and yips of coyotes at the lake.
Hearing them never used to make me nervous
but now everything feels like a threat.
More than once we have seen small packs of them
running together in the distance.
George stiffens and growls, but always stays with me.

I don't like to be gone from the house too long
in case a rescue party comes and doesn't find us.
We limit our outings to riding around
looking for someone left behind.

We don't find anyone.

Laundry

Twenty-one days since the evacuation.

Bottled water supply's running low.
Only enough for a few more days.

I need clean underwear
but don't want to waste water.

I drag the big two-wheeled cooler
out of the garage and haul it to the lake.

Tip it on its side and fill as much as I can.

The water swirls with dirt and muck.
A sodden duck feather floats on the surface.

I use both hands to drag the cooler home.

Wash my clothes in the front yard.
Lay them in the sun to dry.

Use the dirty water to flush the toilet.

Scavenging

I go house to house
searching for food, water, other supplies.

Sometimes doors are unlocked. I walk right in.
Other times, I find an open window or a dog door
big enough to crawl through.

Lots of homes have doors from their backyards
into garages, and then unlocked doors from
garages into houses.

Must brace for the worst.

Many dogs and cats have starved to death
and are decomposing inside.
I occasionally surprise a pet who's managed
to survive by drinking toilet water.
But as guilty as I feel, I can't help them.
It's hard enough to keep George and me fed.
I leave the doors open and try to shoo them through
so they can test their luck at survival outside.

Mostly, though, rancid fish tanks, bird and rodent cages
carcasses of pets make me gag and want to run.
I get in and out as quickly as possible.
Limit my searches to kitchens and pantries.

Anything I haul home has to fit one of
two categories or it isn't worth my time:
1) <u>food and drink</u> (cans of soup, vegetables, fruit, chili, boxes of
    crackers, bottles of water, cranberry juice, ginger ale)
    2) <u>supplies for survival</u> (soap, propane, matches, candles,
        boots, sunscreen)

I always bring a pad and pencil with me.
I always leave a thank-you note with my name and address.

At one house, I find a shoebox full of batteries
along with extra flashlights.

At another, I find a first aid kit with bandages and those ice packs
that freeze when squeezed hard enough.

At still another, I find a hand-cranked emergency radio.

Radio

No news since the power went out.
Only voice I've heard is my own, talking to George.
Or my mother's—calling in my nightmares.

I sit on the floor.
Pull the radio out of the case.
Hold it in my hands, turn it around.
Switch it to on but nothing happens.

How does it work?

Crank the handle several times.
Broken hisses come from the speaker.
Stop again when I stop cranking.
I crank and turn the tuner at the same time.

At first, just static.
After a while, though
words push through the crackle.

Turn the dial back and forth.
Music.
The melody catches in my throat.
Makes my eyes sting.

Turn again.
Voices become discernable.
I don't recognize names or places.
Have no idea where they are.

Sports scores and laughter.
Jokes about a baseball game from the night before.

How can baseball season continue
with so many people displaced?
Are the Rockies still playing somewhere?

More laughter.
Sadness balloons in my chest.
Voices marvel at the events of the game.
I lean back against the wall and cry.

A commercial for Magic Car Wax comes on and
diamond jewelry "guaranteed to win her heart."

A woman reports that traffic is jammed downtown
due to a broken water main.
Commuters should avoid the interchange
at Hudson and Parkway.

The voices sound so close
but they could be as far away

as Maine or Florida or Alaska.
Or Mars.

I stop cranking.
I tuck the radio in my backpack.

Write the homeowner a thank-you note
and head for home.

Ghost

I'm hot and sticky.
I've spent most of the afternoon scavenging.
One more house then quits for today.

I crawl through a large pet door.
Am assessing the contents of the kitchen
when my eyes land on a photo on the fridge.

The face of my classmate smiles out at me.

Heather Juay and I had known
each other since kindergarten.
We were never super close, but we went to
birthday parties and played on soccer teams.
We were friends.

In the summer between fifth and sixth grade
her family was driving in the mountains.
A rockslide fell down on the highway
crushing the roof of their car.
She died instantly.

My whole family went to the funeral.
I occasionally saw her brother at school.
Now I am standing in her kitchen

her dead face grinning at me from
the front of an appliance.

Heather's bedroom is easy to find.
It's as though no time has passed.
Like she might walk into the room at any moment.
Bed made.
Stuffed animals arranged across the pillow.
Movie posters on the wall.
Summer reading books stacked on the desk, along with
a new binder, a ream of notebook paper
a package of mechanical pencils.
Either Heather had been excited to start middle school
or her mother had been.

But the evacuation happened and she's still dead.
Her room stays frozen in time, despite the disappearance
of everyone she loved.

Do ghosts haunt places? Or people?
If she haunts this house
does she know she's been left behind?

I am a ghost.
Haunting this town.

Snoop

I ride ride ride
toward Emma's
neighborhood.
A golf course meanders
around streets called
Enclave and Aerie
and Repose.

Em's ground-floor bedroom
has French doors
out to a fountain and
a trampoline.
The doors are unlocked.

My eyes adjust to the dim light.

Unmade bed.
New clothes with tags still on them
strewn across the floor.
She left in a hurry.

Bottles of nail polish and polish remover
on the plush carpet next to
a pile of stained cotton balls
and a stack of magazines.

In the bathroom
cosmetics litter the counter.
A hair dryer in one of the sinks.
A bottle of Emma's perfume.
I remove the glass stopper.
My throat cinches shut.
The fragrance is so familiar
it's disorienting.
Like Emma is standing next to me.

I see myself in her mirror.
My face is sunburned and my hair
hangs over my shoulders in tangles.
I haven't worn makeup or
straightened my curls since
the evacuation.
I'm wearing Mom's T-shirt
with the lotus flower and the om symbol
but it's stretched and faded and
smells like lake water.
My shorts are filthy and
I haven't shaved my legs.
My silver Converse have a hole
in one toe.

Emma would not approve.

I lie on her bed.
Bury my face in her pillow.
I can smell her shampoo.
Sleepovers and slumber parties.
Salted-toffee popcorn. Pink lemonade.
Cold feet under down comforters.
The time Emma dreamed she was
standing up in a canoe and
fell out of bed
in the middle of the night.
We got the giggles.
Couldn't stop laughing.

Where is she now?
Is she laughing somewhere
with someone new?
Does she ever think of me?

Too Personal

I go upstairs.
The house comforts me
despite the lack of human presence.

In Emma's mom's office
a large desk takes up two walls.
I swivel in her plush leather chair.

Pile of documents
under a glass paperweight
with tiny flowers inside.
Folder labeled
Dissolution/Divorce.

This can't be right.

Emma's family is officially
the Happiest of All My Friends.
Emma's dad gives her mom
beautiful, expensive presents.
Whisks her away
to remote Caribbean islands and
exclusive Swiss chalets.
They kiss in public
even at school events.

The whole family
counts their blessings
before eating dinner together.
Every night.
Literally.
Counts them.
Before anyone takes
a single bite.

I go back downstairs.
Out into the backyard.
Lie in the shade under the trampoline.

If Emma's parents aren't happily married
I'm not sure a happy marriage is possible.
My own parents fought and cried
before they finally split up.
Emma's never mentioned
anything like that.

Does Emma know?

Has the evacuation changed anything?
Made them forget their troubles?
Or has it made things worse?

I want to unread everything.
Go back to Perfect Happy Family.
This is too personal.
Intimate.
Especially if
Emma doesn't know.

I want Mom.

Nothing Makes Any Kind of Sense

i ride.

pressure
in my chest
starts as
a low thrum
but swells from
inside out
emanating from
belly upward
pushing against
sternum
into
throat
taking space
in my
mouth.
sound
bursts out
up into
air above
the road.
shouts.wails.roars.
down below
muscles

explode
pedals
blur.

i ride
as
fast as
i can
straight
down
the middle
of the
street

toward
home.

Dream

I'm at Heather's funeral
but my parents are getting
married and I'm
shouting at them to stop
and I'm trying to find
Jennifer and Paul
and the twins are crying
and I look into the grave
and see Trevor playing
on top of Heather's coffin
and I scream
but nothing comes out
and I wake up
in the middle of the night
jaw clenched fists locked
shaking violently.

Paradox

maybe God
sends us nightmares
so our living reality
doesn't seem so bad
when we wake up

until we wake up
and remember
we are living in a nightmare
we can't escape
except by going
to sleep

I Want to Know More

I sit at Paul's desk.
Open drawers.
Shuffle through files.
Bills. Tax documents.
I find what I'm looking for.

Mom's divorce papers.
I want to know what really happened.

Fifty percent custody.
Alternating holidays.
Shared costs of orthodontia and college tuition.
Take turns claiming me as a dependent
whatever that means. Ironic given
how independent I've become lately.

Paul's files are boring, except for
a bunch of ten-year-old hospital bills
and brochures about in vitro fertilization.

Wow. Seriously?

Never occurred to me
that the twins weren't just
freaks of nature.

I'm glad Paul and Mom had Trevor.

As much as I resent sharing my room
    (It's only . . . just temporarily, honey, until
    we get the basement finished . . .)
I adore the slobberface.

Photographs

A shoebox full of photographs
on a closet shelf.
Some taken before my parents got married.
College. Graduate school.
One from when they eloped in Las Vegas.
I love my mom's jeans and T-shirt.
My dad's long, curly ponytail.

Baby photo of me in a
tie-dyed onesie snuggling a lamb.
Pretty darned cute.
Mom must've enjoyed dressing me up.
Different outfits in every photo.

Dad seated at the piano.
Me standing on the piano bench.
Leaning on his back
making us both laugh.
I pull that one out.
Set it aside.

School photos.
Happy holiday faces
around Christmas trees.
Can't remember some of those

early years together
just as a family of three.
Now impossible to imagine life without
Jennifer and Paul and Trevor and the twins.

Hate stories about wicked stepmothers.
The phrase "broken home" pisses me off.

At my sixth-grade back-to-school night
the principal told all the families that
"children from broken homes were five times
more likely to suffer mental issues than those
where the family of origin was intact."
Mom got so angry she cried.
Afterward, Dad told the principal
to do anatomically impossible things
to herself on her way to hell.

Maybe once the evacuation order is lifted
we can write a book about our lives.
Or something.

And maybe
Emma's family will be okay
too, after all.

Homesick

I take a baby photo of me
reading and cuddling
in Mom's lap and
the photo of Dad
and me at the piano
out on the porch.
Sit and study
my parents' faces.

Close my eyes.
Picture them safe
somewhere.
Together.

Mom and Dad talking intently
to high-level military
personnel who strategize
about how to get back
to Millerville to rescue me.

Jennifer playing with Trevor
while Paul and the twins
consult with top military brass
on expediting homecomings
for all evacuees.

I smile
thinking my family might
single-handedly halt
the *imminent threat*
and save the day
for me and the rest
of the country.

I wonder who will
play us in the movie.

It's Weird

The *imminent threat*
all the reporters
were talking about
has yet to materialize.

At least that I can see.

Aside from the power going out
nothing has changed.

It's weird
not having a device
to turn to
with every urge
to text someone
go somewhere
know something.

my body's habits
    reaching
    clicking
    swiping
    bending
    over my screens
are breaking

my muscles are confused
but
my mind is steady

Days. Weeks. Months.

Weeds choke
the yards
in all
the neighborhoods
and grass
grows tall
and goes
to seed.

Dogs and cats
roam
the streets
foraging for food.

The summer
crawls by
and the
evenings begin
to cool off.

I talk
to the silence.

Sometimes
I sing.

I study
my features
in the mirror
looking
for traces
of my family.

I don't recognize
my face
but
I see
my father
in my
hands.

Comfort

Sprawled out on Mom's bed
in the glow
of solar garden lights
wedged between
the headboard and the wall
I reread her worn-out copy
of *Mrs. Mike* for the
gazillionth time.

Perfect escape from my reality.

Possibly the best
adventure-romance-fiction
book ever written. Never fails
to transport me out of my life
and into the vastness
of Mrs. Mike's
Canadian wilderness.

Follow the geese north
over Millerville toward Wyoming
over Montana toward Alberta.

Toward Sergeant Mike Flannigan
Royal Canadian Mounted Police
in his red jacket with brass buttons.

Sergeant Mike and me.

Facing unrelenting threats of danger.
Fighting to survive against all odds.

Doesn't matter I am far
from family and
luxuries of civilization.
Together we can overcome and
together we will. Together we do.

I close the book
curl up on my side
and sleep the sweet
peaceful sleep
of fantasy.

Teenager

September 28.
I wake up early.

I know it's my birthday because
I've been marking the days
on Mom's calendar.

126 days since evacuation.

Jennifer and I had planned a big
shopping trip for the perfect
teenager outfit.

I nudge the sleeping dog.

George opens one eye
blinks at me, lets out a loud
sigh and closes it again.

I don't need his help.

I pull out Mom's evening gowns
and hold them up.
Dark blue with
rhinestones scattered

across one shoulder and
down the back.
I slip it over my head.

Slide into a pair of Mom's
fancy strappy heels.
Too high and
too pinched.
Flip-flops are better.
My feet don't show.

I shake my hair out
of its braid.
Pin it to the top of my head
in a glamorous updo.

I dig through Mom's vanity.
Rhinestone choker.
Fancy cocktail ring.
Old-fashioned, sparkly
clip-on earrings.

I put on eye shadow
and blush.
Line my lips
the way Emma
taught me.

I'm a movie star.

I stand in front of
the full-length mirror
and strike a
Katharine Hepburn
pose.

George cocks his head.
He sees the improvement
over my usual
post-evacuation fashion.
No dystopian
lack of style
today.

Today
I'm a teenage
goddess.

Sometimes I act younger
than I am, but
I don't care.
There's nobody
here to see.

As the only human
resident of
Millerville, Colorado
I can do
whatever I please
on my
birthday.

Visitor

George sniffs around
doing his business
and I promenade
my finery through
the backyard.

Dry, brittle tufts
of grass catch the
tulle underskirt
and make it
difficult to glide.
Mom and Paul
would die
if they could see
the state of the yard
but what can I do
without water
for sprinklers?

Is Mom recognizing the date?
Trevor turned one already.
Are the twins ten yet?

George growls.

Ten feet away
in the middle of
the backyard
is a coyote.

George barks.
The coyote stares back.
George rushes it.

The coyote hesitates
for a split second
before bounding
over the fence
and disappearing
into the tall grass.

George barks and barks.
Sniffs all around where
the coyote was.

I run up on the deck.
Look in the direction
the coyote ran.
Can't see
any sign of it.

George keeps sniffing
and barking.
Pacing back and forth
in front of the fence
where the coyote
jumped.

I call him to me.
Tell him what a good dog he is.
Hug him.

The coyote was thin
and thin means hungry.
What would he have done
without George here?
What will he do next time?

I joke about the coyote
bringing a birthday-gram.
A singing coyote-gram.

I try to laugh
but my hands shake
and my knees won't
hold me up.

I sit on the top step.
George stands next to me
on high alert.

I nuzzle my face
into his warm side.

Such a good, good boy.

Magical Thinking

Upstairs.
Take off gown.
Pull bits of dead grass and
pine needles out of hem.
Hang gown on padded velvet hanger.
Return to closet.
Replace jewelry.
Rebraid hair.
Pour water on cloth.
Wash face.

Now bathing consists of heating
lake water on the camp stove.
Using a soapy washcloth to scrub
off what grime I can.

Hair is a different disaster.
Most of the time I just keep it up.
Out of the way.

Mom and Dad must realize it's my birthday.
They must be thinking of me.
They could be thinking of me this very second.

What if
right now

at this exact moment
we are all thinking
of one another
at the
exact

same

time?

We could trigger some kind of magical energy in the universe.

The power of our three hearts
missing one another at the same time
would be enough to break
this hellish spell.

I make a wish.

Kneel on floor.
Press folded hands to forehead.
Squeeze eyes shut.

I remember world religions from school.
Imagine Jesus and Buddha and Muhammad
sitting somewhere listening together
to people's prayers from around the world.

I clasp my hands harder.
Concentrate.

> *Please please please*
> *please please please.*
> *Let my parents find me.*
> *Let my parents come home.*
> *Let my parents find me.*
> *Let my parents come home.*
> *Let my parents find me.*
> *Please please please*
> *please please please.*

A warm tongue licks my cheek.
Eyes open onto George's big black and brown face.
He raises one tawny eyebrow. Cocks his head.
I close my eyes one last time.

> *Please please please*
> *please please please.*
> *Amen.*

Rite of Passage

A queer calm comes over me.
It's clear that
for whatever reason
my parents
are not able to
come back.

I am on my own.

To survive until help arrives,
I must rely entirely on myself.

This birthday is not about
evening gowns
dressing up
playacting.

It's time to stop fooling around
with childish games and
superficial nonsense.
Start acting like an adult
whose life is at stake.

Childhood is over.

Scissors.
Braid.
(inhale)
Cut.

Chop
until short spikes
bristle all over
my head.

I coil the long braid in my hand.
It feels alive.

I wrap the braid in
my mother's silk scarf.
Tuck it into the vanity.
Under the mirror.
Out of sight.

I look down at the dog.

Time to get serious.

Change of Strategy

I've stayed close to home
all this time, certain someone
was coming to find me.
Not wanting to miss them
when they came.
Now staying alive is top priority
even if it means going beyond
the neighborhood.

There's no telling when my parents might return.
There's no telling when my parents might return.
There's no telling when my parents might return.

If I say it a lot maybe I'll start to understand it.

The days are cooling off.
Getting shorter.
I need to think about the immediate future.

On hikes, Dad always harped on how fast
the weather changed in Colorado.
How we needed to be prepared.

With no electricity and no furnace
I need to plan for what could be a cold, lonely winter.

It always snows before Halloween.

There's no time to waste.

Hunter-Gatherer

On patrol with George.
Our eyes are open for the coyote.
Nothing.

Abandoned cars sit
in the supermarket parking lot
like islands in the middle
of an asphalt ocean.
People pushing carts of groceries
will emerge from the gaping
doors at any moment.

Inside, skylights provide dim illumination.
Smells of rotting food, urine, feces.
Impossible to breathe.

George's nose twitches.
Fur on the back of his neck stands at attention.
Hair rises on my own arms.

A toppled display of cookies and cakes.
Plastic boxes chewed open, contents eaten.
Overturned candy racks.
Half-eaten wrappers.

The dogs have been here.

Eyes straight ahead.
Hands on cart.
Navigate around dog mess.
Try not to breathe.

Five jumbo jugs of bottled water.
Three cases of canned dog food.
Dog treats.
Chew toys.
Canned fruits.
Canned vegetables.
Canned chili.
Canned spaghetti.

I don't bother leaving a note.
I have stopped thinking in terms of imposing
on other people's property.

I think only of survival.

Ant (not Grasshopper)

It takes
forever
to get home
pushing
the big heavy
shopping cart
and
stopping
to rest
along
the way
but
by visiting
the store
every day
for a week
I am able
to restock
the pantry
with
plenty of food
for me
and George
as well as
drag in enough

water
juice
and
energy drinks
to last through
several
blizzards.

I unpack the last load of supplies
and park the empty shopping cart
around the east side of Mom's garage.

I exhale.

Exhausted
from
winning
a race
I didn't
even
know

I was

running.

Heat

I've made a critical mistake.

No wood-burning fireplaces on Lake Drive.

The houses are designed
with modern, gas-operated ones
that turn on and off
with the flick of an electric switch.
Useless.
They don't even have chimneys.

No fire, no heat.
No heat, no way
we will survive
a Colorado winter.

We Have to Move

Dad's house has
an old-fashioned woodstove
in the living room.
We often use it
in winter to help
heat the downstairs.

But Dad's place
is in Old Town,
twice as far
as the trek
from Mom's neighborhood
to the supermarket.
The shortest route involves
walking around the lake
on gravel trails that
will not be easy
pushing a shopping cart
full of supplies
over and over again.

Without heat, we'll freeze.
Without food, we'll starve.

It's already getting colder every night.
Time is running out.

We have to move.

Plan B

Thirty yards down the lake path
toward Dad's house
the full shopping cart
bogs down in the gravel
and won't roll.
Rocking makes it worse.
Rocks jam the wheels.

Riding back and forth
with the bike trailer
would be faster, even though
it can only haul a fraction
of what's in the cart.

Back to Lake Drive.

Mom's minivan looks at me
from the driveway.

Do I dare?

    What if
    I can't
    even manage
    to back it

out onto
the street,
let alone
make it
all the way
to Dad's house
and back?

WhatifIgetintrouble
fordrivingunderage?

I had better dare or there
will be more serious consequences
than illegally crashing
an abandoned car
in an abandoned town.

I shut George in the house
and take the keys.

Driver's Ed

I unlock the driver's door
grab my bike helmet
and climb in.

Safety first.
I buckle my seat belt across my lap
and click my helmet strap under my chin.

I turn the key.
Surprise and hallelujah!
The engine starts.
The gas gauge points to
a third of a tank.

I grip the steering wheel.
Try to slide the gear shifter into reverse.
It won't move.
I try again.
It stays put.
Surely it isn't supposed to take this much force.
There must be a trick.

Think.

Why would it stay in park?
What's the advantage of that?

Safety first!

I press my foot on the brake pedal and try again.

The gear shifts easily into reverse.
I whoop a victory whoop.

I ease my foot off the brake
and the car begins rolling backward
down the driveway.

I turn the wheel and overcompensate
so the rear end of the car backs up
on the front lawn.

Pushing down hard on the brakes
throws me backward in my seat
and the car stops abruptly.
I sit for a minute, choking on
my heart in my throat.

At least it's facing the right direction now.

I keep my foot pressed on the brake
slide the gearshift into drive
and inch down the street.

I circle the block four times before
I feel confident enough to risk
George's life too.

I pull back into the driveway
and start loading up the van.

Define Home, Anyway

I used to change houses
every Monday

(homecoming
        cominghome)

routinely reunited
with one parent
routinely separated
from the other

a member of the
Divorce Nomad Club
making the weekly switch
according to the
custodial agreement.

This is different.

Mom's new, modern
neighborhood
three-car garage
(cold)

Dad's one-hundred-year-old
farmhouse
heirloom rosebushes
(warm)

Empty houses aren't home.

Woodstove

I've seen Dad light fires many times
but I didn't pay close attention.
I've never done it myself.

The last thing I need is
to burn the house down.

I've got to do research.
Before Evacuation
I had my computer.

So now . . . ? Think.

Before Google.
Before Wikipedia.
Before Internet.

"Come on, George.
We're going to the library."

Millerville Public Library

Front entrance is locked.
I try every other door
but no luck.
In the back by the loading dock
I find a basement entrance
next to a tall, thin window.
I choose a heavy rock
from the landscaping
and heave it.
The sound of shattering glass
shocks the silent town
and I jump
forgetting for a moment
there's no one to chastise me.
No reason to feel guilty.
I reach through pieces
of jagged glass and
unlock the door.

Inside
we make our way
through dim light up to
the main floor and
rows and rows of books.

We pass the children's section
where I spent hours
making crafts and singing along
at Sandman Story Time.

We pass a bank of computers, all dark
and an entire section of CDs, DVDs
and recorded books. Worthless
without power.

In the main section, eastern light
from a big bank of windows
illuminates the stacks.

I walk down rows, reading labels
on ends of shelves.
Fiction goes on forever, and then
magazines and newspapers.
Finally, nonfiction, but everything's
organized by random topics and
numbers on spines don't make sense.

How am I ever going to find a book
about how to light a fire?

"Okay, George. We're going to have to go
row by row and check every shelf.

I'll start over here and you start over there
and let me know if you find something."

George wags his tail and follows me.

Books about knitting and crocheting.
Gardening and building birdhouses.
Sailing and travel. History and politics.

Finally, a small section on camping.
No books about lighting fires in woodstoves
but one with a chapter about building and
extinguishing campfires.
I tuck it under my arm and head for Teen Fiction.
George trots along beside me.

We browse novels until we're armed
with enough reading to last several weeks.
Jandy Nelson. John Green. Elana K. Arnold.
Jason Reynolds. Laurie Halse Anderson.
In a state of emergency, there's no limit
on the books we can borrow.

Outside the service door, we surprise
a feral cat sniffing around the bike trailer.
Her angry hiss startles me and
I jump and drop my books.

George tells her who's boss and she dashes off.
We load up our treasure and head for home.

Thank You, Laura Ingalls Wilder

I won't take survival for granted
and I have no intention of being stuck
in a Long Winter with no fuel.

My driving improves
(I still wear my helmet
and seat belt every time).

I fill the van with firewood
from neighbors' yards.
Unload it into high stacks
on the front porch and around
the side of the house.

I read the camping book cover to cover
and practice building fires in the stove.
I scavenge a case of matches from the store
and seal the boxes in plastic baggies.
They have to stay dry no matter what.

I debate driving east
out of town
looking for others
or the edge of the evacuation.

But how would I get gas?
What if I ended up stranded and lost somewhere?

I remember all the Little House stories
where people took chances in winter
and almost perished in the cold.

I could die in a blizzard far from home.

Dad's voice echoes in my head.

Stay put.
Stay put.
Stay put.

Five and a Half Months

Occasionally
on the crank radio
I pick up a signal
from a town
in a state far away
but more often than not
all I find is static.

When I do find a station
I listen for any mention
of the *imminent threat*
or any plans
to end the evacuation
but I never learn anything
beyond what I heard
that very first week.

Often I lie in the dark
at night, wondering
if what I am hearing
is prerecorded.
Nothing ever sounds
current or specific.

When I let the radio fade
the night noises mix
with the static in my head.
My ears strain against
the silence, hungry.

Darwin

Trapped
in the corner
of an alley
between a garage
and a dumpster
a rabbit shrinks
trying to be as small
as possible.
Three dogs
bark and growl.
I ride briskly in the
opposite direction
but I can still
hear the rabbit
when it
screams.

Winter Storm

Freezing rain and wind
take the last of the leaves
still clinging to the trees.

Snowstorms shriek all night
and the house shudders.

I push and drag my mattress
into the front room.
Snuggle with George
under layers of quilts
warm and cozy by
the woodstove.

We keep other doors
in the house closed
to contain the warmth.
I melt snow to wash.
Use bottled water
to drink and cook.

I treat myself
to hot cocoa
in my stepmother's
favorite blue mug.

To Pass the Time

I play solitaire like my grandma does
with cards spread across the ironing board
lowered down in front of the recliner.

I sketch portraits of George.

I read library books.

I ask Trivial Pursuit questions and try to guess the answers
before I flip the cards over to see if I am correct.

I pull out Dad's chessboard and play against myself
rotating the board at each turn.

I watch the snow pile up in the yard
and marvel at the magic
winter still works on the world.

Winter Refugees

Wherever my parents are
and whether or not
they know by now
that I was left behind
there is surely
no hope of rescue
while winter is in full force.
Roads will be impassable
and airports abandoned.

"We're ghosts, George.
Ghosts in a twenty-first
century ghost town."

Short Days, Long Nights

Following each storm
the sun emerges and
melts the snow enough
to make venturing out possible.

I need to save gas and
I'm afraid of driving on icy roads
so we explore the town on foot.
Check neighboring houses.
Look for food and firewood.

Mostly, though, days are cold and dim.

We sleep a lot.

Conserve batteries and propane.
Even though I think we have plenty
to last until the roads melt and clear
I feel superstitious taking
anything for granted.

I read all the library books I borrowed.
I invent a new card game using
three decks and a pair of dice.
It takes several days to win.

I browse the books on my parents' bookshelves.
Read about how to tune a piano.
What really caused the breakup of the Beatles.
The history of Czechoslovakian theater design.

I study Jennifer's field guides.
Choose my favorite wildflowers.
Imagine hiking across a meadow with my family.

I fantasize picnics on mountainsides.
Make imaginary deviled eggs.
Sprinkle dill and paprika.
Top each one with a caper.
I can taste them on my tongue and
feel warm granite under me.

But I learn to be cautious with my fantasies.
They can lead to an ache that begins
deep in my body, fills my torso, and crawls
down my limbs until I can no longer
feel my hands or feet.

Sometimes longing
combines with despair
and leaks from the
marrow of my bones
swirls into my blood

163

permeates my muscles
invades my entire body.

When that happens
it takes all my strength
to crawl into bed
and curl up

wondering
if I can make it
through another
frozen day, still
alone.

Christmas

I drag boxes of ornaments
up from the basement.

Hang shiny balls along curtain rods.

Light the Swedish Christmas candles.
Watch heat from the flames rise.
Little wooden angels spin around in a circle.

I choose more books from the library
and a watercolor kit from the craft section
of the local drugstore.

Wrap them.
Decorate with ribbons and holly.

I find a special rawhide bone for George
and tie a big bow around it.

I make Christmas dinner:
    turkey soup
    canned cranberry relish
    canned squash
    boxed cornbread stuffing with dried apricots
    canned apple pie filling

After dinner, we open our presents.

Sing Christmas carols.
"Silent Night" makes me cry
so we switch to
"Santa Claus Is Coming to Town."

We sit by the fire.
George gnaws his bone.
I paint his portrait.

Think about a holy family
alone in a strange land
wondering
what their future holds.

Trust

Each day
I brush snow off the front porch.
Lay out a row of sunflower seeds.

I sit still and quiet at one end of the porch.

Squirrel comes down from his nest
in the cottonwood tree.
Collects each seed
one by one.

As the days pass
I make the row closer and closer to me.

One day
the row leads right to a seed
in the palm of my hand.

Squirrel gathers the seeds
runs back and forth up the tree
to deliver his treasures.
When he reaches my hand
he pauses.
Grabs the seed.

Is up the tree again
before I can blink.

Every morning after that
he comes right to me.

Eats breakfast out of my hand.

Snow Falls, Melts, Falls Again

The woodpile grows smaller
on the side of the house.

I teach myself "Clementine"
and "You Are My Sunshine"
on Dad's ukulele.

I sing songs to myself.
Tell George stories
about handsome dogs and
brave girls.

Making Art

I spend one whole afternoon
searching through magazines
and catalogs for images of people.
Use my art knife to cut out photographs.
Combine them into different bodies.
Different settings. Different families.
Shellac them onto card stock
and fragments of broken glass.

I hang the installation from the chandelier
over the dining room table.

Air currents move the families
slightly on their strings
but they never tangle
or cross or meet.

One Morning

I unlock the front door.
Let George out.
A spot of color on the ground.

A bright purple crocus peeks
out of the muddy snow.

Over the next days, more crocuses
holler up from their winter beds.
We count and greet each one.

Then yellow daffodils
followed by a rainbow of tulips
up and down the street.

By the time the irises
send up their spiky stalks
spring is official and
a new sense of hope
blooms in my heart.

Peril

(n.) grave risk; exposure to injury, loss, or destruction; danger

Menace

I pedal my bike down the dry-enough road.
Steer around places still coated with icy mud.
Avoid potholes.

We're heading to Bullseye.
Need new shoes and jeans
to replace the ones I've outgrown.
Dog food, propane, lantern mantles.

George lopes alongside.
Nose in air, sniffing spring.

Around the corner
behind the post office
George freezes.
Growls low and deep.

"What is it, buddy?"
I wheel around.
Come back where he has halted.
Fur on the back of his neck
stands straight up.

A car door slams.
Wait—a car door slams?
Incomprehensible.

Dismount. Turn in circles.
Look for an explanation.

Something crashes.
Metal hits metal.

I cry out.
Run toward Main Street and
the certain presence of other humans.

Almost to the corner.
Explosion of breaking glass stops me hard.
A cry of pain.

Is this the *imminent threat*?

A man's angry voice.
"Keep whining about how tired you are
and next time I won't just break your nose."

I stay frozen with George silent beside me.

The same angry voice barks orders.
"Let's go! Come on, move it!
Back that truck up here and get it loaded.
We gotta be over the border by dark."

Gears grind.
The *beep-beep-beep* of a truck in reverse
echoes off buildings.

Other men's voices rumble.
Shout to each other.
Metal hits metal again.

"Let's go! Let's go!
Pick up the pace, you morons."
Angry Voice is closer.

I move into shadows.
George follows.
We slip down the alley.
I grab a bit of muddy clothesline.
Tie George to the fence.
He whines but I tell him to shush.
He sits down.
Cocks his head.

I inch around the side of the building.
Men shout.
Call to one another.

I peer over a windowsill
into the appliance store.

See across the showroom and out
through the display windows
to the street beyond.

Angry Voice has a shaved head.
Mirrored sunglasses.
Combat boots.

His scalp is tattooed
with a skull tangled in thorns.

Other men push heavy appliances
through broken display windows
to a moving truck on the sidewalk.
Their heads are also shaved.
Ink stains their arms.

They aren't careful.
They shove and stack appliances.
Cram as much as possible
into the truck.
Throw smaller items
into the bed of a pickup
parked in the street.

Blood gushes from one man's nose
but he keeps working.

More glass breaks.

Two men come out of the Antique Attic
with a cash register.
Add it to the rest.

Angry Voice shouts from the sidewalk.
Points up the block.

"You two—head over to the pawnshop.
Grab anything we can fence
or sell for scrap.
But no serial numbers!"

The men run.
Chains on their boots rattle.

I crouch down beneath the window.
Hide behind an air-conditioning unit.
I am sure they can hear my heart
sledgehammering my ribs.

I stay still.

On the One Hand

These men are not government or military.
Not a rescue squad.
They remind me of rioters
I saw on the Internet.

What did he mean by fence?
And why no serial numbers?

When they finish looting the street
will they start on neighborhoods?

On the Other Hand

They also remind me of the pastors
at the megachurch. The ones with
Carhartt work clothes and hipster tattoos.
Shaved heads don't necessarily equal danger.

These are the first people I've seen in months.
They have the power to get me out of here.
They might have cell phones I can use.
Give me a ride to an evacuation center.

Then again, it seems like they're breaking the law.
If they know I've seen them stealing
they might not help me at all.

If they turn out to be dangerous,
I have no protection against them.

If they're creeps as well as thieves
I could be in much deeper trouble
than I can ever escape.

Can't Think Straight

Think.
Think.
Think.

All my thoughts are
questions. None of them
are thoughts.

> risk?
> rescue?
> help?
> safety?
> criminals?
> danger?
> assault?

A voice shouts from up the street.

The Deciding Factor

"Hey! Check out
what we found
in the pawnshop!"

I spy.

A man jogs back to the group.
He holds a tiny kitten, mewing and squirming.

"What the hell?"
Angry Voice looks at him like he's crazy.
"What exactly do you plan to do with that?"

"Keep it? It's kind of cute.
It can ride in the pocket of my jacket."

Angry Voice looks at him.
Holds out his hand.
"Lemme see it."

Takes the kitten.
Holds it.
Picks up a towel from the truck bed.
Wraps the kitten tightly.

Swings the towel twice up over his head
and slams it hard into the side of the big truck.

Tosses the towel and its contents back to the man.
Turns and shouts orders at the others.

The man holds the towel.
Nothing moves.
He tosses it into the dirty snow.
Climbs into the back of the truck.
Helps muscle a dishwasher on board.

These are not my rescuers.
If I'm not careful,
I will need to be rescued from them.

I inch back down the alley
to where George waits.

Please Don't Bark, George

We sprint away.

Thank God
there isn't enough snow
to leave tracks.
We dodge in and
out of shadows.

I want to go back for my bike
but can't risk being seen.
I hope if the looters find it
in the street
they will think it abandoned
in the evacuation.

At Dad's house
I lock the doors.
Run upstairs.
Peer down through curtains
to the street below.

Nothing moves.

(So glad I didn't make a fire this morning.
No woodsmoke smell.)

Mind rips through possibilities.

What if they go looting house to house?
What if they find me?
What if they hurt me?

Breathe in. Exhale.
Breathe in. Exhale.
Breathe in. Exhale.

One thing is clear.
I need to know what's happening.
I need to see and know for sure.

I have one advantage.

I know where they are
but
they have no idea
I exist.

Reconnaissance

Dad's black sweatshirt.
Jennifer's black jeans.
Black stocking cap.

Feed George.
Scratch him between the ears.
Good boy. Stay.

Lace up boots.
Slip out back door.
Lock.

Run toward Main Street.
Stay in alleys.
Between garages.
Stop frequently to listen.

I hear them before I see them.

The looters have progressed
farther down the street and are
at the Park-n-Ride.

They hoist up barrels
of cell phones

dump the phones into
the back of the pickup.
Metallic waterfall
of plastic and glass.

Angry Voice leans
against the bus shelter.
Lights a cigarette.

I drop to my hands and knees.
Crawl on my belly under a hedge
of forsythia bushes.

Peer through branches.
Men toss empty barrels aside.
Reach for others.

Angry Voice barks.
"Come on, you idiots, move it!"

He swears.
They hustle to pick up the next barrel.
He flicks the ash from his cigarette.
His eyes glance over ads on
the side of the shelter.

My heart stops.

Right in plain sight
taped to the bus shelter
faded from winter
is my sign from last May
announcing I am here.
Begging for help.

I freeze as Angry Voice's eyes
read over my words.

> HELP! HELP! HELP!
> I WAS LEFT BEHIND AND
> MISSED THE TRANSPORT!
>
> PLEASE CALL!

He turns.
Scans the parking lot.

I press myself lower into the ground.
Pray the bushes will keep me concealed.

He fishes a phone out of his pocket.
Turns back to my sign.
Dials.
Reads something on the screen.
Puts the phone back in his pocket.

Reaches into the moving truck.
Binoculars.
Climbs up on top of the cab.
Peers through the lenses.
Scrutinizes the entire area.
360 degrees.

A man with a tattooed neck calls up to him.
"That's the last of them."

He lowers the binoculars.
"Right. Load up then."

Trucks roar to life.
Men climb into a passenger van.

Angry Voice slides down from
the roof of the cab.
Climbs into the driver's seat.
Flicks his cigarette into the gutter.

All three vehicles pull out onto Main Street.
Accelerate in the direction of the interstate.

I stay frozen until I can no longer hear
the rumble of the biggest truck.

Once it has been silent for several lifetimes
I roll onto my back and exhale.

Tears roll down my cheeks.

I didn't know it was possible to be
relieved and devastated
at the same time.

After

For days afterward
I have trouble sleeping.

What-ifs haunt me.

I'm terrified to think
what might have happened if
they'd found me. But still
not convinced being found
would have been all bad.

Any sound makes me jump
out of my skin.

I wait more than a week before
I start using lights again at night.

I find my bike where I left it.
Ride cautiously through town.
Survey the damage the looters did
to all the local businesses.

Broken windows. Broken doors.
Destroyed property. Huge messes.

But now access to stores is easier for me.
I am oddly grateful as I go in and out
filling the bike trailer with supplies.

In the little jewelry store
smashed display cases
empty of watches and silver
and pearls.
In the back room
toppled tables and chairs.
Someone tried and failed
to pull the safe out
from under the counter.
Looted workbenches.

I open drawers, looking for tools
supplies that might come in handy.

There, in a bottom drawer
under issues of gemstone magazines
and a six-pack of pocket tissues
I find a handgun.

Black and large and heavy.
I hold it in both hands.
I whistle.

Would I be capable of using a gun
against those men? To protect myself?

      shattered glass
           fresh blood on a white T-shirt
                 a little bundle in the dirty snow

Yes.

He killed a kitten without blinking an eye.

Absolutely, yes.

I will do whatever it takes
to stay alive.

And I have no idea what
the outside world
is becoming.

I search all drawers and cupboards.
Find bullets on a top shelf
behind cleaning solvents.

I wrap the gun
in my sweatshirt.

Tuck it into the bike trailer along
with the ammunition and
other supplies.

I mount my bike and ride on.

Annie Oakley

The first time I fire the gun
the noise and kick of the blast
make me bite my tongue.

I find a library book about
the safe use of firearms.
Practice loading and unloading.

Lock George in the house.
Shoot cans and bottles
in the back alley behind Dad's garage.

Find George hiding in the coat closet.

My aim improves.
I can hit my target more often
than not.

Spring Rolls Toward Summer

George and I move back
to Mom's cooler
more comfortable house
on the other side of the lake.

I stay vigilant.
Never go anywhere unarmed.
Months go by.
The looters don't return.
Neither does anyone else.

We patrol the town.
Keep an eye open for anything out of the ordinary.
Scavenge food and supplies.

I relax a little.

Stop bringing the gun along
every time we go out.
Leave it at home loaded on top
of the refrigerator.

Ready to grab at a moment's notice.

Had to Happen

I wake up early one morning to pee.
Blood in the toilet.

My first period.

I know what to do from all Mom's
your-body-is-a-beautiful-miracle
conversations.
Find pads under the sink
in the master bathroom.

I'm not afraid, but along with
the ache in my lower back
a familiar weight sneaks up.
Surrounds my heart.

Usually I push the weight down.
Stay focused on the job of keeping myself
and George alive, but this time
I let it wash over me.

This ordinary yet
significant event
finds a fissure

in the emotional wall
I've built.

I miss my mother more than ever.

Getting my period is supposed to be
a rite of passage.

My mom is supposed to make
a big embarrassing deal about it.

Supposed to celebrate that I am
Normal and Perfect
and Becoming a Woman.

In a French film Dad and Jennifer love
the mother slaps her daughter's cheeks
the first time she gets her period.
The mother explains
it's to give her a rosy complexion.
Attract lots of boys.

Ha.

Any crushes I might attract are
who-knows-how-many miles away

and I bet no one has even
thought about me since
Before Evacuation.

Even if they could see me now
they'd never recognize the
wild-looking spiky-haired
girl I have become.

And would they even like me?
Doubtful.

Would Ashanti and Emma?

What would they think of my
thieving and shooting and
driving and disregarding
every law ever made
by the county sheriff
or the fashion police?

Have they started their periods yet?
Were their mothers with them?

Mom could slap my cheeks
until the cows come home and

it wouldn't do a thing to help
my freckled complexion.

I am so tired of holding it all together.

Anything at All

I would give anything
to have a real, live grown-up
take over all the worry and fear and work
that I've been doing for the past year
and just let me fall apart.

I want nothing more than to cuddle up
next to Mom and have her
stroke my hair and sing me to sleep
like she did when I was small.

I wonder for the millionth time
if I made a mistake
not revealing myself to the looters.

What if their toughness was just an act?
What if they had rescued me and taken me to safety?
What if I would already be reunited with my family by now?

If I had taken the chance
all this loneliness and isolation
might have been over months ago.

I'll never know if the risk I didn't take
was the stupidest decision of my life
or the thing that saved it.

But I am alive now
and as painful as it is
loneliness alone won't kill me.

At least I hope not.

Soulmate

George senses my sorrow.
Nudges my hand with his soft nose.
I kiss him.
Press my forehead to his broad brow.
Souls merge and swirl.
Such a good dog.

My lower back aches.
I decide our plan to haul bottled water
from the gas station can wait.

I curl into George's solid form.
Snuggle up against his warm side.
Hum Mom's favorite lullaby until
we both fall back to sleep.

Model Home

One afternoon
we leave the bike
and hike to the far side
of the creek trail.
Wander through a half-built
neighborhood development
left unfinished.

Foundations surround
gaping cellars.
Skeleton frameworks of
ghost houses, waiting for
walls and windows.

At the end of a cul-de-sac
one solitary, finished house with
a sign out front: MODEL HOME.

A model home for model families.

A fist clenches
in my chest.
Catches me off guard.
My ears thrum.
A high-pitched

cicada call of blood
rushes through my brain.

    queasy
    lean forward
    hands on knees
    going to throw up
    going to throw up
    going to throw up
    but then
    maybe not
    maybe just soul-sick
    sick-and-tired sick
    spit-in-the-dust sick

Model Family my ass.

Two-dimensional sticker families
on the back windows
of minivans, jeering at
the divorced kids riding behind them
in the car-pool line.

Stick figures brandishing
totems of ecstatic idiocy—

coffee cups and golf clubs
soccer balls and pom-poms

Where is the sticker stepkid
with her sticker suitcase?
Hauling between sticker weeks
back and forth
between sticker houses?
Subdividing the twenty-four hours of
sticker Christmas between
four sticker adults and
two sticker street addresses?

A truly model home would need
twice the number of bedrooms
for half the number of children.

I belong to a family
all by myself:
the only intersection
between four parents
who try to make peace
as if peace is a pie
that can be baked
sliced and served at
progressive dinners

rotating the children
from table to table
house to house.

I pick up the heaviest rock I can find
and hurl it through the big front window.

The splintering crash is almost
satisfying.

Building Site

We pick our way through the
half-finished construction
of the neighborhood.
Look for forgotten tools.
Useful items.
Find one house with a plywood ramp
leading to a doorway.

"Come on, George. Let's check it out."

We explore the ground floor and
I imagine what it could look like.
I paint the walls rich hues to match
plush Persian carpets.
I build bookcases on one wall.
Add a window seat to a bay window.

I find what will become the staircase
to the second floor.
There are only slats where steps should be
but they are wide enough to climb
if I use my hands.

George puts his front paws on the bottom
slat but doesn't continue. He barks
as I climb higher.

"Hush, George."

He whines.
Sits down.
Watches me.

I climb up and stand.
Look out over the open floor plan.
No constructed walls yet so
I have to guess where bedrooms
will start and stop.
Holes in the floor suggest a bathroom
but with no walls, interior decoration
is more difficult.

George barks and whines below.

"Good boy, George. I'm coming. Just a minute."

In the minute I say "minute"
lightning blinks across the sky.
Thunder rolls and rumbles
in the distance.

George barks again.

"Oh, Georgie, it's just a little
thunderstorm. Don't be such a baby."

George yelps.

The wind kicks up.
I shield my eyes from blowing sand.
"I'm coming, boy. Don't worry."

I make the top of the stairs
and glance at the sky.
Dark storm clouds.
A thin gray finger forms in the distance.
Points down and then pulls up again
teasing and poking at the ground beneath it.

Crap.

The tornado touches earth.
A cloud of dust and debris flies up around the funnel.

"George!" I shout, climbing down.
I fight wind and hail.
George barks.
Runs back and forth.
"Let's go!"

Come On, George

We run to the doorway.
Down the ramp.
Slip on wet plywood.
Land in mud at the bottom.
Look around for shelter.
Everything is exposed.

The MODEL HOME sign blows past me.
Slams into the foundation.

"George! Make for the house!"

We plow through the mud.
Run down the street to the cul-de-sac
with the lone house at the end.
The sky is guacamole.
I glance over my shoulder.
The tornado is closing the distance between us.

"Come on, George!"
I put my head down against the hail.

We reach the backyard.
Run to the door.
Locked.

See window wells open down
to basement rooms.

"Come on, George!"
I run for the nearest well.

At the edge of the grass, my foot catches.
I smack down hard on my hands and knees.
Pain sears through my left leg.
Blood gushes from a gash in my shin.
Sharp landscape edging
drips sticky red.

George barks again.
The tornado roars.
I drag myself the last five feet.
Lower my legs over the edge.
Drop six feet to the ground below.

"Come on, George!
Attaboy, you can do it!"
George whines.
Puts his front paws over the edge of the well.

I start to cry.
"Come on, boy! Please, George!"

He puts his head on his paws.
Looks down at me.

The wind is deafening now.
The air is full of debris.
I turn to the window.
Try to slide it open.
Locked.

I shift my weight onto my hip.
With my good leg, I break the window.
Reach around and unlock it.
Slide it open and slip through.
I lose my balance and for a moment
I can't tell if I'm falling or dizzy
or both.

I land on the carpet in a family room.
My body is still but my brain still spins.
I can't find George.

The safest place will be a bathroom
close to plumbing and away from windows.
I drag my throbbing leg across the floor
toward a closed door.
Discover two bedrooms and a closet
before I find the bathroom.

Crawl to the bathtub.
Pull myself over and inside.

The last thing I hear before I pass out
is the crash and shatter of the windows
upstairs imploding.

Consciousness

My neck hurts.
I moan and shift position
but I'm trapped
in something hard and cold.

I open one eye. All is white.

Pain stabs when
I try to sit up.
Turn my head.
I'm in the bathtub.

It's completely silent.

I survived.

Equilibrium

I don't know
how long
I was unconscious
or how long
the storm lasted
but a dim glow
from the family room
suggests
it's still daylight
outside.

I pull myself to a seated position
and on the floor next to the bathtub
is George.

Head on his paws
he tracks me with his eyes.
Wags his stub of tail.
Gazes up.

I try to stand
but the pain in my leg
surprises me.
I fall backward.
George stands up and presses himself

against the bathtub.
Looks at me. Barks.

I lean over and put my weight on him.
Balance on one leg.
He braces me as I shift forward.
Maneuver over the edge of the tub.
Mission accomplished.
I lie, panting, on the bathroom floor.

"This could be a long day, buddy."

Injured

The gash on my leg looks like
a canyon cut by an angry river.
Crimson. Striated. Raw.

A trail of blood leads from
outside the bathroom door
across the floor and into the tub.

I pull decorative towels off the towel rack.
Take off my T-shirt and rip it into strips.
Wrap a towel around the wound on my leg.
Cinch it with strips of shirt.
Wearing only my sports bra and shorts
I struggle to stand.
Even with George's help, I can't walk.

"I'm gonna need a crutch or something, George.
We've gotta find a first aid kit and I'm betting that
Model Homes don't have anything that useful in them."

Room inventory:
   a vase with silk flowers
   a scented candle on the back of the toilet
   a floral shower curtain hanging from a shower rod

A shower rod.

Held in place by nothing more than a spring
and some tension. I smile.

"There's my crutch, George."

I gather the shower curtain in both hands.
Scoot on the floor to the middle of the room.
Brace my good leg against the tub.
Pull as hard as I can with both hands.
The rod pops out. Falls down with a clatter.
I tear off the curtain.
The rod and George help me stand.

Upstairs, we survey the mess.
Shattered windows.
Draperies and paintings in tatters.
Furniture upended.
Kitchen cupboard doors hang askew
on their hinges.
The front door
that had been locked before
has vanished.

We hobble onto the front porch.

Where before there were at least
a dozen half-built house skeletons
now there is nothing.
Not a single two-by-four or
piece of plywood remains.
The only indications that this land
had ever been intended for a neighborhood
are the gaping cellar mouths every fifty feet.

"Holy crap, George. We're lucky to be alive.
I guess this really is a Model Home."

First Aid

The sun is high in the sky.

We limp along for what feels like hours.
Tree limbs litter the streets and sidewalks
but nothing else in town appears damaged.
We head north toward the drugstore.

The looters helpfully broke the lock on the door.
I move the brick I had wedged there to keep
animals out after my last shopping expedition.

I make my way down the first aid aisle.
Sit to nurse my wound.
Blood has dried and caked on the towels.
I bite my lip to keep from crying as
I pull off the makeshift dressing.

Before Evacuation, I would get stitches.
Little point in thinking like that now.
I pour hydrogen peroxide onto the wound
and cry aloud from the burning pain.
I curse as it bubbles and froths a foamy pink.

An infection could be the end of me.
I grit my teeth and pour on some more.

When the bottle is empty, I pat the wound dry.
Apply a liberal coating of antibiotic ointment.
Dress it in clean bandages.
Wrap an Ace bandage over the entire thing.

"Okay, George. I think I'm ready for a
guest appearance on *Emergency 911*."

I rub his head between his ears.
"Let's get you some food before we head home."

We make our way to the pet food aisle.
Break open a box of dog biscuits.
George devours them while I drink
a bottle of Gatorade in big, thirsty gulps.
A package of peanut butter crackers and
a Kit Kat bar give me new energy.

I fill a bag with first aid supplies and
see the perfect solution to my problem.
Propped in a big rack next to the pharmacy
is a wide assortment of crutches.
I choose two, adjust them to my height
and begin the arduous walk home.

Fever

My grandparents' apartment
is as far
as I manage to go.

I prop the door for George
to go pee.

collapse on Grandma's bed

wake up achy and hot
dark out

bedroom door spins
on its hinges
slowly
then faster and faster

a red rubber ball
bounces
through the room
ricochets
off ceiling and walls

drumbeats pummel
my brain

I fall backward
but
where the bed should be
it isn't
tumble through space
dizzy
disoriented

George's head under
my hand

I know I need
to drink

Dad's voice
pounds on my eyeballs
"Stay hydrated!"

force sips of
soda left over
from the sleepover
that wasn't

joints hurt
freezing or drenched
in sweat
kick off covers

225

smell Grandma's perfume
on the pillowcases
Grandpa wipes my forehead
takes my temperature

I was almost five
when my parents
divorced
spent long days
and nights
in my grandparents' care

climb the big bed
tuck in under
Grandma's arm
listen to her read
Little House in the Big Woods
Trixie Belden mysteries

now
in my feverish delusions
I conjure them
to care for me
again

Close Call

I sit up.
My wound has soaked through the bandages.
I unwrap it.
The cut is infected and oozing pus.
More hydrogen peroxide.
Antibiotic ointment.
Wrap it in clean bandages.
Fall back into fits
of troubled sleep.

How long do I sleep?
How many hours elapse?

Sometimes it's daylight.
Other times, it's dark.
The stars move crazily through the windows.

Every time I regain consciousness
I'm aware of George at my side.

Finally, my skin is cool.
No more itchy, hot eyes.
I rise up on my elbows.
My head doesn't ache.
George looks up at me from the floor.
Wags his stumpy tail.

"Hey there, buddy. How're you doing?"
He scoots on his belly to be closer to me.
I rub his head.

"Thanks for taking care of me, sweet boy."
I press my forehead to his.
"I don't know what I'd do without you."

He licks my cheek and whimpers.
"You need something to eat, don't you?
Poor baby. Come on."

I get to the kitchen.
Find crackers and canned tuna.
Collapse on the couch to check my cut.

The angry red has faded.
No longer appears infected.
I clean and dress it.
Sit back against the couch cushions.

I'm already exhausted
but relieved.

I've managed to escape another close call.

Autumn

Chill in the air.
Days grow shorter.
I fire up the minivan.
Drive all the way
to SuperSave
for winter supplies.
Back to Dad's house.

Only drive when absolutely necessary.
Conserve fuel.

I walk and bike as much as possible
but the cut in my leg still slows me down.
Puckery pink scar aches.

Reading Project

I am reading
my way
alphabetically
through the
fiction section
of the library.

Rule #1: Skip the book if I don't like the first page.
Rule #2: Quit the book if it isn't interesting by page 21.
Rule #3: Quit the book if there are no important female charac-
ters.
Rule #4: I can read books out of order if I want to.

I have read 147 novels and
thirteen short story collections and
I am three-quarters of the way
through the *B*s.

Like: Louisa May Alcott
Love: Charlotte Brontë

I get Jane Eyre.
We get each other.
We get loneliness.

"I can live alone, if self-respect, and
circumstances require me so to do. . . .
I care for myself.
The more solitary, the more friendless,
the more unsustained I am,
the more I will respect myself."

Jane thinks my thoughts.

I Cling to the Belief That

My parents survived the evacuation.

My parents are healthy and safe somewhere.

My parents must know by now I was left behind.

My parents will not rest until we are reunited.

My parents will rescue me.

My story will have a happy ending.

Almanac

In the reference section
of the library
I find an almanac
with calendars
going back
hundreds of years
in the past
and forward
hundreds of years
in the future.

I plot how many
days and months
have passed since
I was left behind.

If my calculations
are correct
I've been alone
in Millerville for
seventeen months
eleven days
and counting.

Recommended Teen Fiction

The most popular books
on the library shelf
(the ones the girls at school
pass around like popcorn)
provide little comfort.

To hell with these
heroines who have
entire dystopias rooting
for them as they fight
to save the day.

Sure, their parents are
missing in action
but I'd like to see them
try to survive
completely alone
without any help
from friends
or teammates.

Sure, they're brave
most of the time
but they're part
of something bigger

that inspires them
when times are tough.
Their societies are
messed up, but at least
they belong.

Sure, I wish I had
their skills and resources
but I wonder
would they fare
so heroically if
faced with the
vast loneliness
and uncertainty
that is my everyday
experience?

Not likely.

And Another Thing

What about the
imminent threat?
What is so dangerous
or so threatening
that absolutely everyone
had to leave?

Seriously?
Everyone?

Obviously George and I
are just fine.

Unless we're breathing some
invisible poison gas
that takes months and months to kill us
or
an invading army is on its way
in which case they are taking
their sweet time getting here
and I wish they'd hurry up
so at least someone somewhere
would know I'm here.

What did the TV call it?
Operation Relocate Freedom?

What does that even mean, anyway?

Misgivings

The looters said they
had to get to the border.
Which border?

Can I possibly be
the only person left
in the entire western
United States?

I should leave Millerville.
Take the car and drive as far
east as the gas will take me.

Surely I'll find other people
in other towns who have also
been left behind or forgotten.

Take the chance.
Venture out.
Seek help.

If only
I could be sure

there was someone
out there to find.

And the person won't be
a dangerous criminal
or a psycho kitten killer.

If only
I could be sure
I would survive.

Then Again

I've been across eastern
Colorado and Kansas
and there is nothing but miles
and miles of farmland.

What if the car runs out of gas
in the middle of nowhere?

And even if
I could get to a farmhouse
it would likely be
abandoned with limited
supplies of canned foods
and no bottled water.
I would starve if I didn't
freeze to death first.

And even if
I didn't run out of food
or gas what if I surprised
more looters?

Or came upon
the ever-so-mysterious
and oh-so-dangerous

threat to national security
that caused the evacuation
in the first place?

First Best Chance

Staying put is my first best chance
of being found and rescued.
The risks if I leave are too great.

When frightening thoughts creep in
I will force them aside and visualize
my parents coming to find me.

> I picture them driving in cars or flying in planes.
> I imagine them coming on foot or on horseback.
> I sometimes even imagine them flying across
> the prairie in a *Star Wars* landspeeder.

> No force in the universe is strong enough
> to keep them apart from me.

All George and I have to do is stay alive
and we will be found.

Winter

Overnight
the brown, wet world
transforms
into a frozen white
frostland.

I pull on my stepmother's snow gear.
Mine has grown too small.

"Come on, George! Let's go!"

I trample an icy path to the back shed.
Drag out my father's snowshoes.
We stomp through the drifts.
Head up the road toward the lake park trail.

Not a single creature has disturbed
the sparkly crust of snow.
A glittery reminder of just how alone
we really are.

The only sounds we hear
are our own heavy breaths
and the whish-whish of snow pants
striding back and forth.

George bounds ahead.
Darts back.
Leaps up and down in the drifts
like the lambs that used to play
in the pasture
next to my elementary school.

I throw a snowball.
He catches it in his mouth
but it explodes on impact.

Up and on we trudge
cresting the summit of the trail
to find Miner's Lake frozen
and twinkling before us.

On the snowy surface of the ice
tiny rabbit prints scamper
from one shore to another
despite the owls and coyotes
that hunt here.

We follow the trail circling the lake.
Stop to listen to the snowy quiet.
Breathe the sharp, cold air.

A shadow moves on the ground.

A raptor's silhouette soars in the sky.
We hunker down to watch.

The bird circles the lake
lower and lower
until I see
white feathers on its head and tail.

Bald eagles often winter here
but I have never seen one
this close before.

The eagle catches an updraft
rises in the air
turns and glides down
lands on the ice
just a few feet from the unfrozen center.
Poses there
majestic and still.
So still in fact
I think it has fallen asleep.

My legs cramp from squatting.

Then the bird bursts open
and lifts off
clutching a fat fish

in its talons.
Wings its way up
over the treetops
out of sight.

I Can Almost Pretend

In Mom's neighborhood
the overgrown yards
and gardens
previously wild from neglect
are neat and tidy
in their winter coats.

The houses look cozy
and comfortable
belying their frigid
empty interiors.

I can almost pretend
it's just an ordinary
snowy morning.

The rest of Millerville
is still asleep.

The most extraordinary event all day
will be one eagle's spectacular catch
and the premature death of
one unlucky bass.

Book Report

It feels wrong
to traipse through Mom's house
tracking snow on the carpets
but it's too cold to take off my boots.

I think my mother would understand.

I walk through the rooms
checking windows
are latched and locked.

Everything seems in order.

In the dining room
a piece of paper sticks out
from under the cabinet
against the wall.

Elliott's book report on
Island of the Blue Dolphins.

KARANA THE CHALLENGE GIRL

In the book <u>Island of the Blue Dolphins</u> there are three possible thesises to prove which is the girl's biggest challenge. One, is that Karana has to defend herself against wild dogs. Two, is that Karana must provide food and shelter for herself. Three, is that Karana must learn to trust a friend. Obviously the answer is two, because if she doesn't find food and shelter she will die and then the other challenges don't matter. This is why the answer is defiantely two. But there's another thing that makes her the Challenge Girl. She has to be alone on the island for 18 years!!! That's the total amount of life that my brother and I have been alive if you put our lives together and add them up. That's a very very very very long time. I agree that of the three choices the most important challenge is the food and shelter one, but I think if I were the Challenge Girl, it would be even harder for me to be alone for all that time. I mean, she can always fish and get food and it isn't hard because its her island already. But she has to keep herself company and give herself pep talks and if she's sick or scared she can't just call out to her mom to come take care of her. So I think that's what makes her the REAL Challenge Girl and not that other stuff. But if I have to choose from one of those three only, I guess I still choose two.

Grief

my tears smear the ink and run
across the title
I blot it with my scarf
the paper blurs

Elliott was right.

I was too stupid and self-centered
to even realize it.

food and shelter are nothing
compared to the challenge of
never holding another person's hand
never hearing another person's voice

staying alive isn't easy
but it's a heck of a lot easier than
keeping my heart hopeful and
my mind focused
on what's
real

loneliness and insanity
are twin houseguests
and
it's hard to entertain one
without inviting the other in
as well

Regret

My mind spins with memories.

So many times I was rude
to my stepparents.

How I stiffened when Mom
tried to kiss me good night.

All the times I opted
to stay in my room
alone
sulking
rather than join Dad and Jennifer
for a movie night.

I'm ashamed.

I would give anything
just to see them
hear their voices
touch their hands.

And Elliott.
His handwriting sings
into the emptiness

of my heart.
He and James must be eleven by now.
Do they ever think of me?

"But she has to keep herself company and give herself pep talks. . . ."

Nine-year-old Elliott's words float before me.
He is so smart.

I do have to give myself pep talks.
I do have to keep myself company.

Karana did it for eighteen years
and she was rescued.
When it finally happened
she wasn't crazy with loneliness.
She was excited.
In her best dress and her jewelry
she walked proudly down
to her rescuers
taking her animals with her.

She was triumphant.
Not a victim.

"Stop feeling sorry for yourself
Madeleine Albright Harrison."

I startle George.
He looks up from the rug where he was dozing.

"My parents didn't name me after
the first woman secretary of state
so that I'd turn into a pathetic
pile of poo at the first sign of trouble.
I haven't survived this long and
worked this hard only to fall apart over
a fourth-grade homework assignment.
I need to pull my sorry self together
and get out there to enjoy this
beautiful day."

I fold Elliott's book report and tuck it
into the pocket of my parka.

After Months of Snow

warm breeze
snow melting
trees and rooftops drip
drip drip
open windows
fresh air
buds sprout on limbs
crocus crack through icy earth
i can't help but feel hopeful

Spring Cleaning

Out back
a cool shadow from the house
protects a wide snowbank.

I pack Jennifer's largest cooking pot
with snow.
Set it on the wood-burning stove.

I bathe myself in hot water.
Wash my hair.
Refill the pot.
Wash my clothes.
Hang them in the warming air to dry.

I pull apart my bedding.
Shake out blankets and comforters.
Drape them along the picket fence
to breathe the fresh spring weather.

I pretend to be Laura Ingalls Wilder
in *Little House on the Prairie.*
Sweep the whole house.
Wipe down the surfaces.
Wash away grime and grit

from a winter of closed doors
and woodsmoke.

After a long season of hibernation
my body likes the heavy chores.
The change in the weather and
the strength in my muscles
spark new courage.

What If

What if I've been wrong
        to think that staying put is the best option?

What if it will be years
        before anyone will return to town?

What if forces beyond their control
        prevent my parents from coming for me
        no matter how much they might want to?

AND

What if there are people
        closer than I realize?

What if there are people like me
        who were left behind in Denver?

What if they are living
        as close as thirty miles away?

If I can figure out a way to travel safely
with minimal risk

it can't hurt to venture out
and explore.

Can it?

Is it worth using up the gasoline in the minivan?
Is there a way to take gas from other cars left behind?

What if I get lost?

What if I find people and they turn out to be dangerous?
What if I run into the looters?

What if there are other dangers
        like wild animals
        I might not be able to defend against?

What if?
What if?

What if?

Curiosity Wins

Gas is too precious to waste
on a trip that might amount to nothing.

I try other cars with neighbors' keys.
All dead.

I don't know how many lonely winters might lie ahead.
If I lose the use of the minivan, packing in
needed supplies will be much more difficult.

BUT

that doesn't mean exploratory trips are off the table.
Denver's too far to venture by bike
but Lewistown and Peakmont aren't.
Lewistown is closer, but Peakmont is bigger.

Might have folks like me
who were left behind
OR
supplies that could be useful.
Peakmont has a hardware store.

As soon as temperatures are consistently warm enough
I'm setting out to see what I can discover.

Strength and Conditioning

I begin a daily routine by lifting Dad's free
weights and taking long walks, then long runs
through the neighborhoods.

I ride my bike all over town, choosing routes
that take me up long, winding hills.
I gain strength and endurance and
so does spring.

By the time the forsythia boughs erupt
in their lavish yellow blossoms
and the early redbud trees bloom dark pink
I am ready to tackle a long-distance trek.

Sojourn

Pump up bike tires.
Load pump and patch kit in bike trailer.

Pack food and water.
Rain gear and first aid kit.

Feed George and shut him in the house.
The trip to Peakmont is too long and
I will be riding too fast for him to keep up.
Debate taking him along in the trailer
but that will slow me down.
Need space to bring back supplies.

Strange leaving Millerville.
Since the evacuation, I haven't ventured
farther than the edge of town.
Since the tornado, I don't even go that far.

Pedal north along the highway.
Exposed and vulnerable.
Four lanes stretch out
wide and straight
disappearing in a point.
A vanishing point.

I hope not for me.

A sign tells me I am thirteen miles
from my destination.
Twenty-six round trip.

Farmland lies fallow and untended.
Fields where horses and cattle used to graze
are empty. No sign of animals.

Occasionally, I pass a farmhouse.
Perfectly normal from a distance
but no laundry on the line.
No chickens in the yards.

I think of fresh eggs and milk.
Just my luck to have concert musicians
for parents instead of farmers.

I press on.
Everything is still.

Except for hawks circling the sky
I am the only movement
on the entire landscape.

Pass the Christmas tree farm
and the private school
up on the hill to the west.
Debate riding up there
to scavenge in their kitchen.
Decide to wait for the ride home
if I have the energy.

Up ahead, finally,
the first buildings of Peakmont.
The sun shines high in the sky.
Pull over in cottonwood shade.
Snack on almonds, dried apricots, water.

Ride slowly into town
watching hoping dreading
signs of life.

Business District

I park my bike.
Pull one of Dad's hiking poles
out of the bike trailer.
Unscrew and extend until
it's almost four feet long.
The sharp tip clicks
on the sidewalk.
If anything threatens
I want to be prepared.

I walk down Central Avenue.
Looters were here, too.
Smashed windows and
broken merchandise.

Damn.

I should have brought the gun.
I forgot about it over the long winter
and now it's too late.

Personal belongings
flattened and discolored
by two winters of snow and mud
litter the streets.

Probably dropped or lost
in the evacuation.

For hours I ride through town
senses keen and tuned
to humans
but no whiff sight sound taste.

Hardware store on the south side.
I smash the glass front door.
Crawl in and out, loading up
with batteries and propane canisters.
That alone makes the trip worthwhile.

In the pet aisle, I miss George.
This is the longest we've been apart.
I stuff bags of rawhide chews
and a squeaky, plush parrot
into my backpack.

Dogs

Leaving the hardware store
I hear a low growl.
I freeze, crouched halfway in
halfway out of the door.

A pack of dogs.
Different breeds and sizes
including a German shepherd
a boxer, and several mutts.
One looks like a wolf, but
there are no wolves in Colorado
are there? Could it be a coyote?
Several wear collars.
The German shepherd
bares his teeth.
Growls. Takes a few steps
toward me.

I stay frozen.
My sharp hiking pole
is in the bike trailer.

The other dogs advance.

If I move too quickly
I will cut myself
on the shards of glass
around the broken door.

Even back inside
there is nothing
to prevent the dogs
from coming in after me.

I need an advantage.
Buy some time.

On the floor to my left
is a gumball machine
under a wall-mounted
fire extinguisher.
On the sales counter
is a display of key rings
a March of Dimes donation jar
and a case of beef jerky.

I shift my weight
to avoid the broken glass.
Pull myself back into the store.
Open the case of beef jerky.
Grab fistfuls of dried meat.

The dogs bark, break into a run.
I squat back down.
Throw pieces of jerky as far
as I can out the door.
The first dog devours
one of the pieces.
Sniffs the ground for others.
The pack fights over the jerky
and I throw out more.

While they are distracted
I grab the fire extinguisher.
Pull out the pin.
Squat down again and crawl
through the broken door.
Drag the fire extinguisher with me.

The shepherd sees me.
Turns aggressively. Growls.
I shout and aim the nozzle.
Squeeze the handle
as hard as I can.
White foam explodes
over fur and teeth.
The dogs yelp and yowl
when the chemical hits their eyes.
The shepherd whimpers

and runs off
leading the others away.

I drop the fire extinguisher and
sprint to my bike.
Mount as fast as I can and ride
in the opposite direction.
Much harder work now because
the trailer is full of supplies
but I pick up speed.
Soon I am out on the highway
shifting and pedaling
with all my strength.

Getaway

I ride several miles before
my chest stops pounding and
my breathing evens out.
I can't stop looking back
but the dogs are nowhere
to be seen.

After much time and distance
I slow down.
Fall to my hands and knees
on the side of the road.

Throw up twice.

Those dogs could have killed me.
I am so damned lucky.

They could have found me
out in the open with no
means of defense.
Even with my hiking pole, I doubt
I could have survived a pack
of aggressive, hungry dogs.

I find a fresh bottle of water.
Rinse my mouth.

My legs shake so badly
I sink back down and stay
on the ground
sipping my water and
gathering what's left
of my wits.

Equus

I pedal south toward Millerville
riding to beat the sunset.
The highway unfurls like a striped ribbon.

A dust cloud rises up over the knoll.
I coast to a stop on the shoulder.

The ground trembles. Rumbles.
A herd of horses gallops up onto the ridge.
They move as one equine body like
starlings in a murmuration.

I stand astounded.
Afraid.
Amazed.

They veer west and are gone over the hill
and into the distance, leaving me
straddling my bike in dusty silence.

My fatigued legs find new strength
and I giddyup toward home.

Desolation

(n.) deprivation of companionship; emptiness; sorrow; woe

Homebody

Spring wipes
her muddy boots
on the mat and
settles in to stay.
Everything blooms.
Geese migrate north
and we migrate
back to Mom's house.
No more long-distance
treks. No more exploring
without George.
Staying put.
Staying home.

Early Morning

reach back toward sleep
fleeting images of dream
my mother's face
safety. comfort.
images recede
chest constricts
arms wrap around ribs
ribs wrap around hollowness
ignore grief
hope dream returns

fingers of sunshine stretch
over the eastern horizon
touch tops of trees
squirrels scamper
up slender aspens
leap onto roof
tumble and chatter
across shingles

George shoves open the door and
nudges his nose under my grumpy elbow.

"Stop it, George. Go away. I'm sleeping."

He puts his head on the
edge of the bed. Pushes
his big square brow
against my shoulder
and whimpers.

I groan.
"Why do you have to be so pushy?"

He rolls his brown eyes up toward mine.
Wags his little tail.

Sigh.

I stand on the back porch
in my pajamas.
George explores the yard
sniffs around bushes and
occasionally lifts his nose
to smell the air.

A V of Canada geese flies
overhead, honking.

I shade my eyes
watch their descent
toward the lake.

One at a time they stop
flapping their wings until
they are gliding
banking in formation
circling below the treetops
out of sight.

I remember my dream
the palpable mother connection

I wonder if geese
feel connected
in harmony
as they fly.

Is the feeling of being connected to another creature
a universal feeling across species?

Is that love?

Picnic

I need to CHEER UP.
Even George thinks so.
I pack a lunch and
grab my hiking pole.

At the last minute
I shove the gun in my bag.
The next time
I meet a pack of hungry dogs
I want a better weapon
than beef jerky.

We walk neighborhoods
west of the lake
past the supermarket
down the bike path
toward the creek.

George alternates between
running ahead and
trotting along in step
with me.

My heart rate increases.
My spirits lift.

The path leads us away
from neighborhoods until
we are walking along
the banks of the creek.

Mature cottonwoods
shade the trail.
Damselflies flash
bright blue and iridescent
in the dusty sunlight.
A bull snake slides out
from under a shrub
stretches across the path
slinks off into the grasses
on the other side.

I make George sit and stay
until the snake is gone.
Dad taught me which snakes
are dangerous.
I feel lucky whenever
one crosses my path.

I miss Dad.

The creek does a sparkle dance.
A robin flits back and forth

to her nestlings, mouths
open and ravenous.
A great blue heron stands stock still
on the far bank, plumed head
poised like a statue, waiting
for unsuspecting fish.
Three turtles sun themselves
on a partially submerged log.
A dragonfly buzzes
the surface of the pools
in the shallows near the shore.

We bushwhack down
to the creek bank.
Exhale a long, deep breath.
George arches his back.
Settles down, nose twitching.
We eat our lunch and
watch the creek
tumble over itself.
I remind George not to drink
and pour him some water.
I scratch the spot between
his ears and he closes his eyes
rolling over to offer his belly.
I stretch out, lean on him
and watch the clouds wander
across the sky.

"What does it all mean, George?"
George picks up his head.

I put a piece of grass between my thumbs.
Whistle.

"Is there something I'm supposed to be doing that I'm not?
Is it my fault we haven't been rescued yet?"

Really Truly

I am not particularly religious.
Never given much thought
to whether God exists let alone
whether God pays any attention
to my little life.

Lying on my back
in this beautiful place
surrounded by
so many wild birds and animals
I'm trying to really truly
understand
how alone we are.

This day.
Like a million other days I lived
Before Evacuation.
Like any minute a cyclist will come
riding around the bend.
Or a pair of runners will jog right on by.

The animals around me
are living their lives
just as they always have.
Nothing has changed for them.

Do I look as natural to them
as they do to me?
We're all just trying to survive.
Does that make me wild?

Can one lone girl be a civilization
all by herself?

Two whole years and
I haven't seen another person
since the looters left town.

Is there really no other human being
for hundreds of miles?
Or thousands?

How long can this last?

What would I be doing right now
at this very moment
if the evacuation
had never happened?

a freshman in high school
maybe taking honors classes
studying for final exams
shopping for a dress to wear to a dance

kissing someone for the first time
maybe
or
playing on the soccer team
scoring the winning goal
state championship match
being lifted onto teammates' shoulders
paraded across the pitch in victory
my whole family cheering
jumping with pride.

I reach into my pocket.
My brother's book report.

"But there's another thing that makes her the Challenge Girl.
She has to be alone on the island for 18 years!!!"

Eighteen. Years.
E.I.G.H.T.E.E.N. Y.E.A.R.S.

Am I capable
of surviving alone
for eighteen years?

Trevor would be out of high school by then.
The twins would be in their twenties.
I would be thirty!

Even if
our food and supplies
could last that long
is it possible
so much time could pass
before people return?

possible?
maybe.
conceivable?
no.

Surely the government
wouldn't need that much time
to address whatever *imminent threat*
caused the evacuation.

George is at least six or seven.
How long do rottweilers live?

The thought of life
without him
is unfathomable.

Everything Is Still

We follow the creek path west
twisting and turning with the water
until unfolding
across a footbridge.

A hawk soars on air currents.
A prairie dog chirps an urgent warning.

We trek up and over a hill
down past the cemetery
to the fork at the road
that leads to Lewistown,
the little neighboring town.

We walk along the shoulder
of the road but soon
realize our foolishness and
walk right down the center
on the double yellow line.

"Imagine, George.
We're part of the Rose Parade
and this line is the parade route.
We have to follow it exactly
until we get to the very end, but

be careful not to step in horse manure.
Think of what those marching
band members have to walk through
when they follow the horses every year.
Kind of hard to march and play a tuba
while watching for horse turds
at the same time."

George prances beside me
glancing up
wagging his stumpy tail.

A few more miles and the yellow line
leads us to the intersection
of the cemetery road
and Lewistown's main street.
South toward the baseball diamond
nothing moves.
North toward the businesses
everything is still.

"Come on, buddy. Let's see what's happening."

Lewistown

the French bakery
the guitar shop
the outdoor ice-skating rink

I learned to skate there as a little girl
holding Dad's hands.
Clinging to his legs when
the evening train rushed by
on the tracks east of the rink.

I conjure the hot, sweet scent of kettle corn.
The weight of heavy, wet mittens.

Across the street is the carousel.
Endangered tigers, elephants
sea turtles, arctic wolves.
I circumnavigate the platform
from animal to animal.

George picks his way along
the planks of the floor behind me.
I climb into an old-fashioned sleigh
pulled by two polar bears.

George sniffs the giant panda nearby
then settles on the floor at my feet.

sounds of calliope music
young mothers and fathers lifting tiny
children onto the animals' backs
laughing when the carousel jolts to life

I will the wooden slats in the ceiling to rotate
slowly at first then faster
until I get dizzy and close my eyes.

carousel picks up speed
everything pulls slightly toward center

world whirls
animals come alive
music grows louder, dissonant
animals growl and snort

carousel twists and dips
drops hard and fast
jerks me awake

Twilight is fading.
The railroad tracks gleam

in the light of the rising moon.
Nearby, a cricket sings.

George lifts his head and cocks his dark ears.

My head still swirls, but the earth
at least, is still.

My muscles remember the pack of dogs
and my senses tune to threat.

I step down from the carousel.
George stands and stretches.
Jumps down after me.

Everything is quiet.
Darkness settles around us.
Even the cricket is still.

"Well, Georgie, we better head home
while we have the moonlight.
I'm sorry I kept us out so long."

George dances a circle and falls into step.
I climb the embankment to the railroad tracks.

We walk in silence watching the moon rise
timing our strides to the span of the railroad ties.
Bats dart and dodge high above our heads.

A great horned owl hoots.
Its mate answers in the distance.

Gravel crunches beneath our feet.

We turn off the tracks and
head toward the path.
Ten more minutes and we are back again
in our own neighborhood
heading for home.

Summer

Oppressive heat.
We sleep in
the basement
to stay cool.
Leave windows
wide open.
Hope for breeze.
The sun pounds
the town.
We stay inside
subterranean, like
prairie dogs in
our underground den.

Worries

Since the tornado, I'm terrified
of getting sick or hurt.

I remember the pantry
at Great-Grandma's house.
The bloated top of an ancient can
of potted meat.
Botulism.
I check every can of food for
bulging or bad smells.

How long do canned goods stay edible?
Do pasta and rice go bad?
Boiling food only adds to my water concerns.

We've finished all the drinking water
from the supermarket.
We're raiding bottled water from
local gas stations around town.

Every time I ride anywhere on my bike
I make a point of coming home with
at least one new case of water.

The supermarket still has
a few jugs of distilled water

but I don't know if it's safe to drink
and I keep forgetting
to look it up at the library.
If things get really bleak
I suppose we'll just have to risk it.

Each day I grow more concerned about
what will happen if
our food and water supplies run out.
I read expiration dates.
Organize our food stores to ration cans
with the longest shelf lives.

I continue scavenging
through homes and businesses
but I worry about the day
those supplies will be gone too.

Every once in a while I find
a vegetable garden still producing
a few carrots or radishes
from earlier seasons.
I cook a pumpkin I find growing
in an old compost pile
but the recipe in Mom's cookbook
calls for baking the pumpkin
before mashing it and all I can do

is chop it up and boil it.
The whole endeavor turns out to be
much more work than I anticipate and
the results don't taste very good.

I search for fresh fruit from
the trees around town
but last autumn
the fruit was either too sour
or too wormy.

It's hard not to worry.

Storm

We are swimming at the lake
when a storm rolls in.
I am in the water.
George runs back and forth
along the length of the dock
barking at me.

We both hear thunder.
Clouds amass above the foothills.
Jagged lightning divides the sky.
I remember soccer coaches calling
everyone off the field during practice.
The whole team gathered under
the picnic shelter to wait for thirty minutes
before heading back out.

The hairs on the back of George's neck
stand up as more thunder rumbles over us.

I swim to the dock.
Pull myself out of the water.
Grab backpack, towel, shoes.
Run for home.
Hot drops of rain pelt the street.

I fall into the rocking chair on the porch.
Towel my hair.

George whines and looks at the door
asking to be let inside.
I rub him between the ears.

"Oh, Georgie, so brave in the face of looters
and yet so scared of a little thunder."
We retreat indoors.

Conflagration

It rains throughout
the afternoon.
Occasional claps
of thunder and lightning.

The brittle, dry land
sighs with relief
at the welcome showers.

Lightning continues
through the night
patterns of light
on the walls of the basement
where we lie
listening to the storm.

I am shocked awake
by a sudden explosion of thunder
blinding light.

George barks and whines.
I reach for him.
The smell of ozone wafts
through the air.
"It's okay, Georgie. I think lightning

must have struck pretty close, that's all.
That's an awful smell."

I head upstairs
out into the front yard.
The rain has stopped but
the wind is blowing.
No moon.
I can't see until lightning and
thunder strike again
painting everything in a flash
of brilliant clarity and
deafening noise.
Again, the ozone smell fills the air.

An orange light glows in the sky
behind my mother's roof.

I stare.
Try to reconcile moving light
in the middle
of so much darkness.
Then the ozone smell is replaced
with smoke.

"George! It's a fire!"

It Happens So Fast

Back into the house.
Dining room.
Kitchen.
Out into the backyard.

Beyond the fence in the open space
a huge cottonwood tree is ablaze.

A dark scar mars the side
where lightning struck.
Flames lick the branches.
Encircle the trunk.

The wind picks up.
A giant limb crashes onto
the split-rail fence and
the fence catches fire.
Sparks and embers rise
into the sky.
The fire travels.
Engulfs my brothers' fort
in the corner maple tree.
Burning two-by-fours fall to the ground.
Now the maple is ablaze too.
The fire consumes the fence.

Eats its way around
the perimeter of the yard
toward the house.

It happens so fast I don't think
about the possibility
that I might be in danger.
The wind blows in
from every direction.
This fire is famished.
It swallows the length of the fence
then leaps to the Nortons' house.
Within minutes it's licking
their second-story windows.

Sparks blow from the Nortons' house
to our roof.

"George! Come!"

What to Save?

We run back into the house.
Stand there.

I don't know what to save.

family photos?
artwork on the walls?

What meaning does any of it have if
no one ever comes back again?

My water supply and food are in the garage
but the mudroom door is hot to the touch
and I choke on smoke billowing up
from the crack underneath.

The garage is already on fire.

I run back into the living room.
Find my shoes.
My backpack's on the floor
where I dropped it.

I grab it
slam open the front door
and drag George out of the house.

Ashes, Ashes

for hours we're hypnotized
watching our home
and houses up and down the block
devoured, consumed, destroyed

the fire is ravenous
but flames never reach
over here across the street
where we sit paralyzed
in the heat

the wind dies down
the rain resumes
douses everything
drowns the last of the flames

thick, white smoke rises
from burnt-out foundations

skeletons of cars sit
black and unrecognizable
where garages stood

my skin is plastered with wet ash
the taste of smoke coats
my mouth and nose

the sun rises
alien and green
on the smoky horizon

I'm filled with despair
for all I've lost

my brothers' fort
the yard where Mom married Paul
the first home baby Trevor ever knew
obliterated

and my supplies of food and fuel
my mom's van
the bicycle with the trailer
all destroyed

now I am truly stuck here

I can surely find
another bike
but
what are the chances

I'll find another car
that will still start after
two years and
two winters

any flirtations I had with
making my own way
back to civilization
burned to the ground
along with my neighborhood

stand up
limbs unfold stiffly
pull my backpack over my shoulders
tug at George's collar

he lies still on the porch
follows my movements

another tug

come on, old friend
there's nothing here for us now
let's go

he rises slowly
the trauma of the fire has aged us both
overnight
together we walk into the smoky sunrise
toward the lake trail to Dad's house

Aftermath

The smell of smoke lasts for days.
Mom's street is not the only one destroyed.
Lightning caused fires all around Millerville.
Dozens of houses burned.

I have to throw away my clothes.
Even my backpack reeks.
As I empty everything out
my hand closes around something
wrapped in plastic at the bottom of the pack.

A flattened Twinkie.
A fossil from my duplicitous life Before Evacuation.

I stretch out on a blanket in the shade
close my eyes, and eat the spongy cake.

It tastes as if nothing has changed.

Treasure

After Mom's house
is reduced to cinders
I search everywhere
for signs of her.
I scour Dad's house
from top to bottom
hunting for anything
she might have touched.

I find a birthday card
she wrote to Jennifer.
Discover a stash
of my elementary school
tests and reading logs.
Use my finger to
trace Mom's signature
over and over again.

The greatest treasure
is a postcard she
sent me from
Washington, DC,
when I was little.
She printed in
block letters so

I could sound out
the words by myself.

I tuck the card in my
pocket next to
Elliott's book report.
I carry it with me
wherever I go.

Postcard

THE BLOOMING CHERRY BLOSSOMS
MAKE MY HEART HAPPY, JUST LIKE YOU DO.
SOMEDAY I'LL BRING YOU TO WASHINGTON
SO YOU CAN SEE THEM FOR YOURSELF.

I LOVE YOU, MY MADDIE GIRL!

XOXO, MAMA

3/4

Tantrum

Night is the hardest.

I stay busy during the day
gathering food and supplies.

Night, though, my mind is
more busy with fears than tasks.
I try praying a few times
but I feel self-conscious
and awkward.

I find a spiral notebook and
a pen and write a letter
to God instead.

I remember Mom's strict rules for
How to Be a Good Correspondent.
Always start with gratitude.

Dear God,
     Just in case you had anything to do with
it (and if you do actually exist), thanks for
helping save George and me from the fire,
and for helping us find food and water
and all the stuff we need every day.
We appreciate all the help we can get.

Adjust the solar garden light.
Stare at the wall.

Why the hell haven't you rescued me yet?????

Cross it out.
Try again.

~~Why the hell haven't you rescued me yet?????~~

I was wondering if you might be able to give
me some help down here? I mean, if there is
any way you could manage a little miracle and
GET ME THE HELL OUT OF HERE I WOULD
APPRECIATE IT!!!!!!

I mean, seriously, God, am I being tested or
something?? What more do you want from me???
I'm doing my part. I'm keeping us alive. When
are you going to show up and start contributing
a little, huh? Would it really be that hard, in
light of everything else you've supposedly
accomplished?

WHERE THE HELL ARE YOU????
Heat roils in my chest.
I hurl the pen and the notebook

across the room
knock books and knickknacks
off the dresser and
onto the floor.

I storm into the kitchen
open the cupboard
and pick up a stack of
dinner plates.
Slam out the back door
into the dark yard
and throw each plate
as hard as I can
against the cinder-block wall
at the back of the property.

The sound of shattering ceramic
echoes off the neighboring houses.

When all the plates are broken
I run back inside and gather up
as many drinking glasses
as I can carry.

When they are smashed to pieces
I go back once more and
drag out all the empty bottles.

When everything has been
reduced to sharp shards scattered
across the dead grass
I collapse on the back stoop.

The dark braces for more.
Holds its breath.
The ground glitters
with broken glass.

A cricket breaks the silence. An owl hoots.
Another echoes a response.
A bullfrog sings nearby.

A black nose pushes under my elbow.

"Hey there, big guy. I'm sorry if I scared you.
You're going to have to go out to pee in
the front yard from now on.
Too much broken glass out here."

I'm no longer fuming
just exhausted.
I have no complaint with God.
If God exists
it's entirely possible that
I have him or her to thank

for helping us survive
as long as we have.

I can throw all the tantrums I want
and it doesn't change a thing
or bring my parents back.

I am the most ancient teenager
on the planet.

Rebuilding

Everything seems flammable
and we are jumpy and anxious.

George leaves the room whenever
I strike a match.

I raid the kitchen at the megachurch.
Load a neighbor's red wagon
with enough water
to last several weeks
at Dad's house.
Try to rebuild our food stores
but without Mom's van
stocking up for winter
will take much longer.

I pull the wagon
breaking into houses
businesses
up and down the streets
systematically searching
for food
water
firewood

Some houses still smell awful
from the carcasses of
dead pets or rotted food.
Others seem almost normal
as if someone were just there
or stepped out for a moment.

As the days get hotter
I scavenge enough
to feel cautiously optimistic
about our prospects for
surviving another winter.

Can Opener

George loves the can opener
and the bounty it liberates
every night for his dinner.

I do not share his enthusiasm.

After so many months
of eating nothing
but canned goods
fresh food is a memory
I've forgotten.

My tongue has amnesia.

My teeth wouldn't know
what to do with
anything firmer than
a chickpea.

Food is fuel.
Nothing more.

no pleasure
no flavor

Everything cooked.
Everything soft.
Reduced to
salty or sweet.
Indiscernible from one
can to the next.
Only minor variations in
color or texture.

chunky or soupy
mushy or meaty

One night I dream I am eating
a grilled cheese sandwich
with fresh tomato and three kinds
of cheese on sourdough bread.

In the morning, my pillowcase
is wet with drool.

Garden

An idea plants itself in my brain.

Grandpa always had a summer plot
in the community garden.

I ride to their apartment and rifle
through drawers in the kitchen and pantry
until I find a bundle of faded seed packets
held together with a stiff old rubber band.

Do seeds expire?

I spread them on the kitchen table.

Zucchini
Radishes
Marigolds
Carrots
Spinach
Tomatoes
Cauliflower
Zinnias

Read the backs of the envelopes
and am crushed to see

I should have started the seeds
indoors two months ago.
Apparently growing seasons are specific.

Should I wait until next spring?
Is it really possible I could still be here next spring?

Photos on the front of the packets
make my mouth water.
Even the flowers look delicious.

I decide to try half now and
save half for the future
whatever the future turns out to be.

Farmer Girl

Once again the library saves the day.
Provides everything I could
ever hope to learn about how
to plant and tend a vegetable garden.

(Back in civilization
when I grow up
I think I might want
to be a librarian.)

No time to waste so I get right to work.

Use Grandpa's plot for luck.
The garden is so neglected and overgrown
it's hard to tell it was ever anything
but a vacant lot full of tumbleweeds.

I am undeterred.
The thought of fresh homegrown vegetables
wakes me each day like an impatient rooster.

By the end of the week
I am sunburned and so sore from all
the weeding and clearing and digging

and bending and hoeing but I've done it
and my seeds are in.

I write the names of each vegetable
on Popsicle sticks to mark the rows.

I haul water from the lake.

I even make a scarecrow out of an
upside-down rake, a flannel shirt
and a pair of overalls.
The birds don't seem to care
but it scares George.

optimism
satisfaction
pride

Unfamiliar feelings take root
in the soil of my tired soul.

Seedlings

The radishes are sprouting!

I have created life.

I feel like God.

Twenty-Five Days Later

I sit in my garden
on an upside-down bucket
holding a warm, white radish.

I brush away the dirt
and marvel
at how perfectly
exquisite it is.

It smells like earth
and life
and prosperity.

It tastes like euphoria
and hope
and laughter.

the bite
the crunch
the tang
the sweet

I roll it on my tongue
until my stomach

gets jealous and demands
satisfaction.

It does not disappoint.

Watercolor Sky

Starts to drizzle.

There is no thunder or lightning.
It just rains. And rains and rains.

The scorched little town is thirsty.
The cool moisture is a welcome change.
Washes away the trauma of fire and devastation.
Nourishes the growing garden.

Like a blessing.

Deluge

After losing count of rainy days
I hear a sound I haven't heard
in over two years.

Water running in the house.

I look in the bathroom
and the kitchen
half expecting to see
a tap left on
but find nothing.
I go down the stairs
to the basement
which is hardly more than
an unfinished storage space.

Water gushes up
from a drain in the floor.

I grab a bucket
but the thick, muddy water
bubbles in faster than I can bail.
More water pours down the walls
from under tiny basement windows.

It is as if the earth has
drunk its fill and
the rain has decided to come
live with me.
It moves in bag and baggage.

I have no choice but
to watch the water rise.

A Plague of Water

I monitor the basement
constantly.
The water rises well above
the bottom steps
before the rain outside
finally lets up.
I pull on my father's slicker
and Jennifer's rain boots.
Venture out, leaving George
at home safe and dry.

Streets are rivers.
Yards are cluttered with debris.
Hubcaps. Porch furniture.
Broken fence posts.

Everything is littered with
leaves, branches, mud.

Where my garden was there is now a pond.
Popsicle sticks float on the surface.
Ducks paddle around my scarecrow's knees.

The sky is the color
of bruises.
Matches the hue
of my new mood.

Flash Flood

I pick my way to the trail.
Hike up the rise above
the bike path and
look down on the creek.

A stream once narrow
enough to jump across
is now a torrential river
dozens of feet wide
rushing with a ferocity
I've never seen.

Bridges and paths are
washed away.
Fences are pushed over
or gone.
Roads are wiped out
leaving jagged edges of asphalt
like broken teeth in
a gaping mouth.

A red barn door crashes past
spins around
jams against the bottom
of the train trestle

creating new obstacles for
the water to pummel and thrash.
A pair of tractor tires tumbles by
like toys in a bathtub.

I start to back up but
the deep muck wants to suck
the boots off my legs.
I tug my foot
lose my balance and slip
down the embankment
toward the rushing rapids.

I scream
but the roar of the water
drowns my voice.
And there's no one
here to hear me.

Trapped

I grab
at tufts of grass
as I slide
down
the muddy bank
but
my hands
can't
grip
and I fall
into
the
torrent.

I come up
sputtering
head
above water
shoulders out
but
my foot
lodged
between two rocks.

The current
slams me
like a battering ram
against
a concrete
retaining wall.

I'm trapped.

Even as the river
pins me again and again
I feel it
rising.

I have to
get out of here
or
I will
die.

Rope

tree branch
rope swing
big knot draped
over pipe on wall

reach
out of water
up
farther
fingers barely
graze

too high

one foot stuck
one free
brace against rock
pull hard
harder

foot won't budge

wiggle toes
in boot
wiggle pull

wiggle
pull
pull
pull
foot starts
to slide

cry out
deep breath
pull
more until
foot
escapes boot
water slams body
against
wall

breathe

brace
feet on rocks
count three
push
up
reach
stretch
up
reach

rope unhooks!
swings
way out
across river
away

water slams body

watch
arc
breathe
wait
brace
push
reach

grab rope!
hold hard
tight

pull
push
climb
push
climb
pull
pull

push
up
out
up
out

to safety

Wrung Out

I drag
hands and knees
up
the muddy bank.

Collapse
in the
soggy grass.

Exhausted. Shivering.

Ghost water still slams me
slams me against the wall.

My muscles don't know I'm safe.
I'm safe.
I don't feel safe.

I can't hear anything
over the rush
of the angry flood.

The din and vibration of the rabid river
expand into my chest and my throat.

Grief presses on the backs of my eyes
and blinds me.

I wail
hugging myself
rocking.

Of Course

of course
I am alone
so no one
hears me cry
comes to comfort
or help me
of course they don't

they can't
because
they aren't
so of course
they don't

there is no they

the river stole
my boots
my socks

my feet are gashed
and bloody
my hands
are raw

rope-burned
rock-sliced

but there is nothing
to do
of course
except haul myself
up from the ground
and
go home

Parable

Home in bed
embraced in my comforter
curled around sweet, steady George
I remember a parable
from a friend's bar mitzvah.

> *A man who drowned in a flood arrives in heaven,*
> *angry that God didn't save him. God reminds*
> *the man that he sent him rescuers in a canoe,*
> *a rowboat, and a helicopter, but the man kept*
> *telling the rescuers, "No, God will save me."*
> *He was too foolish to recognize God's help.*

It's one thing to stay alive.

I'm managing that with or without God's help.

But how much longer can I stay sane?
How much more can I bear alone?

Elliott's words
float through my brain.

"I think if I were the Challenge Girl, it would be
even harder for me to be alone for all that time."

The challenges of fires and floods
can be overcome with courage and wit,
but this feeling of loss and loneliness
might just prove too great to endure
even for this Challenge Girl.

After the Flood

The world is strange.

A floating propane tank
tumbles downriver
crashes into a boulder
and explodes.

Wild animals
wander through town
disoriented and displaced
from flooded habitats.

And rattlesnakes invade
the neighborhoods
in search of dry ground
after their culverts overflow.

After surviving so much
for so long
I swear
I will not die
from a stupid snakebite
or an encounter with
a mountain lion.

When we're outside
I ring the cowbell
from Dad's bike races.
Stay to the center
of streets.
Eyes peeled
for anything coiled
or crouched.
Ears tuned
for rattles or growls.

When the cold weather finally arrives
and sends the snakes into hibernation
I exhale for the first time in centuries.

351

Another Birthday

I do not celebrate.
Push aside all feelings
about turning fifteen.

Every day is just another
to withstand and overcome.
Every night is just a Pyrrhic
victory of survival.

Emma and Ashanti already
had their birthdays.

I didn't remember.

If a birthday falls in the forest
but there's no one there to celebrate
do we still get older?

October

First snowfall.

Ongoing hunt
for food and fuel.

Basement water's gone
but leaves a nasty smell.

The creek
is swollen
but has receded some.

I wonder if it will
freeze completely
or flow
through the winter.

Acceptance

(n.) the act of believing; coming to terms
with something; recognition

Sanctuary

I love the library.
My own personal book church.
Safety.

But I'm losing patience with fiction.
The challenges and triumphs of
fictional characters only make me
feel worse about myself.
Novels end nicely and neatly
with all obstacles overcome.
Loose ends tied up.

My own story just keeps unraveling
with a depressing predictability.

In fourth grade, Mrs. Hawkins taught us
three kinds of literary conflicts:
    humans against humans
    humans against nature
    humans against themselves

I don't need to read novels to understand
the challenges of human survival.

Don't tell me about tragic heroes on epic quests.

I am Penelope
weaving the days away
waiting for Odysseus
to return.

Emily

I hated poetry in school but for some reason
I love browsing in the poetry section.

There is something about poetry
being nonfiction
but not factual.

The most intimate personal thoughts
—things people would never dream
of saying out loud in middle school—
right there on the page in black and white.

I choose books based on the titles
and whether the poets' names
sound like people I might like.

e. e. cummings is a rebellious teenager
who refuses to follow any rules
and Billy Collins is an eleven-year-old kid
who lives next door.
I wonder if T. S. Eliot is a man or a woman.

One day
I'll go to college with poetic friends
sit in coffee shops

write stories about
the olden days of the *imminent threat*
the trials and tribulations
I endured.

I want a poetic friend to keep me company
explore alongside me
help me forage for food and fuel.
I run my hands along the spines
looking for women's names.
I find Emily Dickinson.

The book falls open.

> *"Hope" is the thing with feathers -*
> *That perches in the soul -*
> *And sings the tune without the words -*
> *And never stops - at all -*

Well, that's true.

I have never stopped hoping
my parents will come back for me
or at the very least
someone will pass through town
and rescue me.

But there are many days
when the act of hoping
feels even more difficult
than the never-ending work of
gathering food and fuel.

If Emily Dickinson is right
and
hope is a bird perching in my soul
then my hope hovers
on the verge of flying away
at any moment.

Mary

With Emily in my backpack
I move farther down the aisle
to *New and Selected Poems*
by Mary Oliver.

The woman on the cover
gazes at something out of view
as if she doesn't know
she is a poet and
she is being photographed
for the front of a book jacket.
She looks pensive.

I open to a random page.

>   *The Summer Day*

>   *Who made the world?*
>   *Who made the swan, and the black bear?*
>   *Who made the grasshopper?*
>   *This grasshopper, I mean—*
>   *the one who has flung herself out of the grass,*
>   *the one who is eating sugar out of my hand,*
>   *who is moving her jaws back and forth instead of up and*
>   *down—*

who is gazing around with her enormous and complicated eyes.
Now she lifts her pale forearms and thoroughly washes her face.
Now she snaps her wings open, and floats away.
I don't know exactly what a prayer is.
I do know how to pay attention, how to fall down
into the grass, how to kneel down in the grass,
how to be idle and blessed, how to stroll through the fields,
which is what I have been doing all day.
Tell me, what else should I have done?
Doesn't everything die at last, and too soon?
Tell me, what is it you plan to do
with your one wild and precious life?

I mark the page with my finger
flip the book closed
so I can study
the author photograph again.
I search Mary Oliver's face for a clue
about what drew her attention
off to the side of the camera.

I open to the poem again
study the words on the page.

> *I do know how to pay attention, how to fall down*
> *into the grass, how to kneel down in the grass,*
> *how to be idle and blessed, how to stroll through the fields . . .*

I have learned to pay attention too.
All the time I've spent
combing this town
for every salvageable
piece of food
bottle of water
possible stick of firewood.
I pay attention to the weather
and the seasons
to what's growing
what's dying
how much daylight is left
in an afternoon.
If I didn't pay attention
I would have
frozen or starved
to death
a long time ago.

how to be idle and blessed, how to stroll through the fields . . .

I've been idle sometimes.
Have I been blessed?
I have certainly been lucky
not to have been injured or killed
to have survived this long alone
despite the fact that I'm only fifteen and

I should be thinking about dating and
homework and Friday night football games
not scavenging for food
and wondering if I'll survive
another winter.

> *Doesn't everything die at last, and too soon?*

Doesn't everything die at last
Doesn't everything die
too soon?

Oh my God.

I can't believe this never occurred to me before.

Is it possible they haven't returned because they didn't survive?

Could they have died not knowing that I had been left behind?

Could they really have died not knowing that I had been left behind?

It makes sense.
As painful as it is to even think the thought
it explains

everything.

novacula Occami

Something must have happened to my parents.
Something *did* happen to my parents.
Otherwise they would have returned by now.

There is no scenario I can dream up
in which my parents discover I am missing
and don't immediately come for me.
Even a foreign attack on the government
couldn't stop them.

A quiet truth grows up from
the core of the earth and into
the core of my body.

I'm not sure how I know, but I do.

I even try to go back to
how I felt a few minutes ago.
Try to believe
they are out there
somewhere
coming for me.

But I can't.
There is no doubt in my mind.

They are never coming back.

Nothing and Everything

The knowledge that my parents are dead
changes nothing about my daily life.
Winter is still coming and
I still have to prepare.

What has changed is my anxiety
and sense of urgency.

They are gone.

I used to worry about
wandering too far from the house
or missing a rescue party
but I don't anymore.
I work hard during the day and
sleep well at night.
No more nightmares.
Sometimes I even sing.

It's not that I don't grieve the loss
of my family or feel the acute emptiness
of being so alone.
It's just that my grief and loneliness
are no longer burdened by hope
that things will change.

I can't control the future and
I'm powerless over everything
except what's happening
right in front of me.

If rescue comes, it comes.
If it doesn't, it doesn't.

Even Still

I can still bathe
in the light of the moon
as it rises huge
and orange in the east
and in the
expanse of constellations
that spill across the sky
on a clear, cold night.
I can still marvel
at a hawk
soaring overhead
with a snake in its talons.
I am still here.

Reconciliation

(n.) the act of restoring to harmony; resolution; reunion

Wild and Precious

I'm officially in love
with Mary Oliver.
I envy the confidence
of her poems
and I draw strength
from the possibility
that I, too, might
one day understand
my place in
the natural world.
I am certain
that the question
she asks at the end of
"The Summer Day"
is intended just for me:

> Tell me, what is it you plan to do
> with your one wild and precious life?

I don't know
what might be in store
down the road
but I know I won't
waste another day
agonizing over

what I can't control.
I am going to make sure
my one wild and precious life
is spent living as fully and
completely as I can
and if that means living alone
with an aging rottweiler
and eating canned food
until I'm an old woman
so be it.

Blizzards

I have to dig a path for George to go out to pee.
Sometimes he just goes in the snow on the porch.

We stay warm by the woodstove.
The storms leave behind a sparkling world of ice.

The sun slices cold through the sharp blue and every tree
twig, stone, fence post is enshrined in glittery prisms.

George struggles on the slick glass sidewalk
but I push off and slide for several thrilling feet.

We play in the wintry beauty until I can't feel my toes.
The sound of my laughter echoes up and down the street.

Spring Flowers

After months of cold
warm weather finally
subdues winter.

Green sprouts emerge
out of the dark, moist earth
and buds appear on branches.

In the front yard
the redbud tree explodes
into thousands of
tiny purple blossoms.

Daffodil and tulip bulbs
push their tenacious stems
up from the ground and
burst into boisterous color.

Purple larkspur grow rogue
and tall from the cracks
in the middle of streets
and sidewalks.

Gaillardia bloom in red
and yellow clusters on

the mounds of rock and soil
that used to be the creek path.

Black-eyed Susans, purple
coneflowers, and multicolored
cosmos decorate alleys, yards
and vacant lots.

It seems the floodwaters scattered
more than debris and destruction.
They also sowed new seeds
in places where flowers
never used to grow.

New beginnings for the battered town.
New beginnings for my weary heart.

Summer Advice

As the days pass
and the light elongates
the temperatures reach upward
and I reach back
to the poets
to Mary Oliver's summer
advice to *fall down in the grass*
though the grass in Millerville
grows riotously long
after so many seasons
with no tending.

I *stroll through the fields*
play with feeling *idle and blessed*
ponder my *one wild and precious life*

Could my life be any wilder?
Or more precious?

If Emily Dickinson's hope
is *a thing with feathers*
then there are many
flocks of hope flying overhead
nesting noisily

in the trees and hedges
all around.

The beginning
of my fourth year
alone in this place
yet Mother Nature insists
on optimism.

Autumn Fruit

Plums fall to the earth in messy
piles of red and purple sweetness.

Apricots and peaches hang like
juicy jewels buzzing with bees.

Apples are so abundant their
branches bow all the way down
to the ground.

In the abandoned garden at
Millerville Elementary School
one enchanted apple tree yields
six astonishing varieties.

I am a fairy-tale princess picking
red, green, yellow, and blush-
colored apples from different limbs
of the same tree.

Teeth break skin. Tongue licks juice.
Shiver-pleasure ripples through me.
Fruit flesh in my mouth.

I eat my fill
and fill my pack.

Interlopers

George wakes up stiff and limping
so I leave him home and trek out alone.

I scavenge among the orchards behind the
retirement villas in my mother's old neighborhood.

I load my backpack and am crossing the street
when a loud rumbling vibrates the ground.

I freeze, unable to translate the sound.
It's my imagination. Has to be.
I close my eyes. Will the rumbling to stop.

But the sound isn't in my head.

The whir and chop of a helicopter comes closer.

rescuedangerlootersinvaders?

Giant's Boot

I drop my backpack.
Run as fast as I can
toward the side yard
of the nearest house.
Throw myself into
a cluster of spirea bushes.
Tuck down into the
smallest space possible.

A Chinook helicopter
materializes overhead.
Its great, gray body
blocks the sun.
Military? Friend or foe?

When I was little Dad teased me
when formations of Chinooks flew over.
I thought they looked like huge boots
with propellers at each end.
Dad made up stories about a careless giant
whose shoes kept flying off his feet.

Engine rumble continues.
Doesn't recede.
I crawl to the front corner

of the house.
The helicopter hovers
over the lake
down past the end of
the street.

I backtrack around
to the backyard.
Skirt the deck. Climb over
the split-rail fence.
Hug the houses.
Keep ears and eyes
on the sky for
other helicopters.
Pick my way from
yard to yard toward
the end of the block
and the west side
of the lake park.

Stay low in the shadows.
Cut north toward
the wetlands preserve.
Scramble over the hill.
Drop and belly crawl
into the willow thickets
on the north lakeshore.

Sneak toward the water
and the sound of
the helicopter.

The Chinook hovers
above the lake.
Creates whitecaps
pulsing out in all directions.
Hangs there several minutes.
Rises up and flies over
the boathouse
on the southern shore.
Lowers down again.
Disappears out of sight.
Red dust clouds the air
and I know it landed
on the baseball diamond
behind the parking lot.

If these are looters
they are far more
sophisticated and prepared
than the men on trucks
years ago.
If they aren't looters
this could mean rescue.
This could be the chance

I've been waiting for
all these lonely months
and years.
But they could also be invaders
from another country.
The *imminent threat*?
Maybe they are the reason
for the whole evacuation
in the first place?

My heart slams back and forth
almost as loud
as the helicopter.
I have to see what's happening
without being seen.

Spy

The east end lake path
is the shortest
but wide open and exposed.
Visible to anyone.
Nowhere to hide.

And whoever's on board
the chopper could just as easily
be coming down the trail
from either direction.
The last thing I want
is to walk straight
into someone
or something
unprepared.

My mind works faster
than my heart pounds.
Keep hidden
no matter what.
It's my only advantage.
Can't risk being seen
until I know
what I'm dealing with.

Stay deep in the willows.
Scramble along coyote paths.
Zigzag through thickets
toward the west end
of the lake.

The sound of the engine
cuts off.

I freeze.

Can't hear anything
but water lapping
on the shore.
My own breathing.

One careful step at a time.
Aware of every sound I make.

Men's voices coming closer.
Can't discern what they say.
Voices grow louder
then shift direction
and fade.

Count to fifty.
Creep to the edge
of the trail.

Peek out as the men turn
away from the lake
toward the east end
of the neighborhood.

Wait another moment.
Dash across the trail
into a stand of cottonwood trees.

And But

I will not let my fear of these unknown men
sabotage what might be my only chance at being saved
AND
I refuse to let my desperate hope for rescue
cloud my judgment and put myself in danger.

How many times have I been tested since the evacuation?
How much more will I have to endure?

Blizzards. Looters. Tornados. Dogs.

Injury. Fires. Floods.

Hunger. Fear.

And the deepest loneliness imaginable.

I have faced impossible obstacles.
Conquered every challenge thrown at me.

Whether these men offer friendship or threats
I can only keep George and myself safe if
I can figure out who they are
and what they're doing in Millerville.

I am afraid of being discovered.
I am equally afraid of losing track
of where the men have gone.

The thought of being so close to other humans
only to be left behind again is nauseating
BUT
the possibility that they might pose a threat
or do me harm is downright terrifying.

From one moment to the next
I don't know which is worse.

Flesh and Blood

follow the voices up the trail
into the neighborhood
keep to the shrubbery
move from shadow to shadow
stay within earshot

at the end of my mother's block
peer around the corner
see them all huddled
in the middle of the street
their backs to me

unlike the looters, these men wear
matching jumpsuits, boots, and caps

they walk up the street
pause to look at burnt-out remains
of houses and cars

I watch
ready to run
at any moment

they stop at Mom's ruined house
one of the men walks forward

shakes his head
pulls a handkerchief from his pocket
blows his nose
turns and
for the first time
I see his face

Her face.

My mother's face looks out
from under the cap.

Her hair is cut short and
her eyes look exhausted
but it's my mother
flesh and blood.

I burst into tears

and then I am running, running and
shouting down the street, shouting
with my entire body and spirit.

My mother and the men turn toward me.

I see nothing but
my mother's stunned beautiful face

as I fly toward her
then
I am in her arms and
we are weeping together
holding each other
rocking back and forth.

She is shorter and smaller
than I remember
but her arms are familiar and strong
and I dissolve into them

    and then another set of arms
    encircles and embraces us both
    and I hear my father's voice
    laughing and crying
    repeating my name
    over and over.

They are here.

They are alive.

They have come for me.

They have come.

After-Words

their voices
their questions
the touch of their hands

everyone's waiting
they say
everyone's fine

the *imminent threat*?
it never existed
a massive land grab
unprecedented fraud
elections
new government
conditions returning to normal

I can't care
not yet
so many answers
too many questions

there is only this

the touch of their hands
skin on warm skin

family skin
our skin
own skin

to be held
to be seen
to be heard
to be known

these are the nutrients
missing
from my diet
of the last three years

mal-love-nourished

forgot totally what it means
to be heart-quenched
soul-satiated

now it fills me
feeds me
holds me
stills me

with George tucked
beneath my feet

and my mother
and my father
each holding
my hands

we fly
up and over
the only home I ever had
the home I forced
to feed and shelter me

up and over
the charred neighborhood
the lake
the park
the town and all its buildings
the houses
the schools
the ruins from flood and storm

down below
my ghost self haunts
a maze of streets
always searching
always hunting
sometimes hoping
always wishing

now there is only this

they have come for me
come back for me
back to this home
this home that tried to kill me
tried to keep me alive

they are here
I am here

simultaneous impossibilities

like everything

like nothing

like love

Acknowledgments

When I was eleven, I visited New York City. I wanted to be a writer and I knew that New York was where many books were published, so I went door-to-door at several of the big publishing houses on Sixth Avenue and introduced myself. I didn't have appointments, but the editors invited me into their offices and talked with me. I left with a stack of business cards and an invitation to send them my stories. That day, I learned that people who publish books are very kind.

I am now much older than eleven, but the people who publish (and write and illustrate and edit and design and sell) books are still very kind, and I am lucky to have met and worked with many of them to make this one. I am so grateful for the keen insights of Kristin Gilson and Anna Parsons at Aladdin, and for the entire team at Simon & Schuster, especially Valerie Garfield, Heather Palisi, Chelsea Morgan, Mike Rosamilia, Brian Luster, Valerie Shea, Emily Hutton, Michelle Leo, and Mara Anastas. Merci beaucoup à Pascal Campion.

Enormous thanks to Deborah Warren for championing the manuscript from the moment it entered her inbox, and to Matt Ringler for his encouragement and support in helping it find its way to Deborah. Thanks to Erin Dealey and all the writers and illustrators who support each other so generously at East West Literary.

Ideas for stories can take a long time to grow into books, and I am grateful to the people who nurtured and encouraged this one.

Thanks to the Mother-Daughter Book Club where the seed was first planted: Leah, Nina, Susan, Olivia, Liz, Alyssa, and Fiona. Thanks to the people who read the manuscript in various iterations and offered feedback: Emma Buhman-Wiggs, Lillian Norton-Brainerd, Heather Preusser, Kristie Letter, Shelby Pawlina, Ginny Downey, Sarah Azibo, Beckie Garrett, Jen Dauzvardis, Alan Freeman, Kathie Freeman, Kim Tomsic, and Leah Rogers. Thanks to Trevor Norton, Garnie Kelly, Mark Ziegler, and Katie Covey for providing technical insights.

I am deeply grateful to principal Melissa Christensen, teacher Dana Reyes, and the discerning students at Peak to Peak Charter School for workshopping the manuscript with me, and to the many other people who encouraged and celebrated each milestone, especially Fiona Freeman-Grundei, Nicole Hewitt, Catherine Hagney Brown, Leah Stecher, Mariamne Friedman, M. D. Friedman, Kelly Reeser, Kristianna Vedvik, Jennifer McKeown, Tiné DelaTorre, and my Texas and California families. And despite the enthusiasm of all these people, this story would not have become a book without the abundant resources of the Society of Children's Book Writers and Illustrators, and I appreciate the Rocky Mountain Chapter more than words can express.

A special thanks to Marti Rolph Rhode for walking up and down Sixth Avenue with me all those years ago. All children need adults who take their aspirations seriously.

And most importantly, to my husband, Rob. Thank you for all you do to make my writing life possible. I adore you.

About the Author

MEGAN E. FREEMAN attended an elementary school where poets came into the classrooms every week to teach poetry, and she has been a writer ever since. She writes middle-grade and young adult fiction as well as poetry for adults. Also an award-winning teacher, Megan has decades of experience teaching in the arts and humanities and is nationally recognized for presenting workshops and speaking to audiences across the country. Megan used to live in northeast Los Angeles, central Ohio, northern Norway, and on Caribbean cruise ships. Now she lives near Boulder, Colorado. Learn more at MeganEFreeman.com.